Metaphorosis

May 2022

Beautifully made speculative fiction

Also from Metaphorosis

Metaphorosis Magazine

Metaphorosis: Best of 20xx
Metaphorosis 20xx: The Complete Stories
annual issues, from 2016

Monthly issues

Plant Based Press

Best Vegan Science Fiction & Fantasy
annual issues, 2016-2020

from B. Morris Allen:
Chambers of the Heart: speculative stories
Susurrus
Allenthology: Volume I
Tocsin: and other stories
Start with Stones: collected stories
Metaphorosis: a collection of stories

Verdage

Reading 5X5 x2: Duets
Score – an SFF symphony
Reading 5X5: Readers' Edition
Reading 5X5: Writers' Edition

Vestige

The Nocturnals, by Mariah Montoya

Metaphorosis

May 2022

edited by
B. Morris Allen

ISSN: 2573-136X (online)
ISBN: 978-1-64076-228-2 (e-book)
ISBN: 978-1-64076-229-9 (paperback)

Metaphorosis
a magazine of speculative fiction
from
Metaphorosis Publishing

Neskowin

May 2022

Indicative of Future Results

C. H. Rosenberg

The Frontpage Feed: Morning Edition.
Carefully curated and fact-checked headlines delivered to your inbox, every day!
SUBJECT LINE: *Extraterrestrials Exposed?!*
Top Ranked News (56,031 shares): *Stunning 'Proof' of Extraterrestrial Cover-Up Floods Internet.*

Yesterday's release of thousands of purportedly top-secret documents by a self-proclaimed former high-ranking national security official sent shockwaves across the metaverse.

The manifesto accused the United States and allied spacefaring nations of covering up an extraterrestrial message received several years ago, when both competing nation-states and private enterprise were emerging as serious contenders in a second Space Race.

The self-described whistleblower claimed a signal was intercepted by a joint scientific team on board the International Space Station (ISS) and the origin later pinned as the TRAPPIST-1 star system in the Aquarius constellation. All media inquiries to the personnel named in the leaked documents were directed to an ISS Program spokesperson who declined to comment.

The manifesto goes on to reveal that a second message was recently intercepted, with analysts agreeing it amounts to an announcement of an impending arrival. "In other words," the alleged former insider warned, "an extraterrestrial vanguard is on its way—we *hope* for the purpose of establishing diplomatic relations. Either way, our leaders are fooling themselves if they think they can keep this under wraps."

While such claims of extraterrestrial contact are typically dismissed as false alarms, several respected experts appear to be taking this particular claim seriously. The International Academy of Astronautics and the SETI Institute both urged calm while they work to verify the purported evidence.

Business and Finance News (4,833 shares): *Closing Bell Round-up*

Personal finance guru Connie Padilla today announced the release of her eagerly awaited book, *Give Your Future Self a Raise*. In this fresh spin on retirement planning, Ms. Padilla, 42, offers her characteristic pragmatic advice, as always inspiring readers with her message of financial empowerment. This adds to a growing media empire so far encompassing a semiweekly podcast and newsletter, two other published books and a robust digital community platform. Ms. Padilla regularly appears on the conference and talk show circuit and recently kicked off a live weekly show, where she answers her audience's questions on everything related to personal finance.

LIBRARY: **Latest**   **Episode.**
Downloading...
Power   Your   Personal   Finance—
UNPLUGGED! *Episode transcript..*
Live streaming in 3...2...1. Cue teaser,
introductory music, sponsor plug

Connie: Hello, hello everybody! I'm *so* glad
        to welcome you here on episode ten
        —*ten!*—of the live stream version of
        Power Your Personal Finance! I'm
        Connie Padilla, Certified Financial
        Planner *and* author of *Give Your*
        Future Self a Raise—out now!— plus
        two other bestsellers, *Power Your*
        Personal Finance: The Fundamentals
        and *The Smart Side-Hustle.*

        Each Friday, I take questions from
        people *just like you*, live on the
        show. My goal is to help you take
        control of your financial future, for a
        worry-free   life   today   and   a
        comfortable retirement tomorrow.

        First off, a quick disclaimer: *Power*
        Your Personal Finance is purely for
        educational   and   entertainment
        purposes. Anything said on this
        show should not be construed as
        individual financial, legal, tax, or
        accounting   advice;   listeners   are
        advised to discuss their personal

financial situation and goals with a financial professional. And remember: while we talk about stocks, bonds, real estate, and other investment opportunities on this show, past performance is *not* indicative of future results!

Now, without further ado, let's get to your questions. And from my inbox, it's pretty obvious what most of you have on your mind.

Sound effect: Drum roll

Connie: Aliens! [*laughter*] Just kidding, folks. But several of you clearly *are* worried about defending yourselves from scammers and hoaxes. So, let's start off with a couple of questions about protecting your personal identity. Then, we'll step back to look at asset protection more holistically.

[*Fast forward.* TIME: 24.59]

Connie: All right, we have time for one more call today. Let's go back to the queue. Hello! Who's this?

Frank: Hello, Ms. Padilla. I'm...Frank.

Connie: Hey, Frank. How can I help empower you today?

Frank: What's the *deal* with personal finance, anyway?

Connie: ...Huh?

Frank: Apologies, Ms. Padilla. I'm just... *frustrated*. Maybe because I'm so new to all this? I mean, I've done my homework, I've listened to your entire archive of episodes, I've read *all* of your books—

Connie: Wow!

Frank: But I still feel completely overwhelmed! I'm usually very good at picking up new things—it's my *job*—so this is pretty embarrassing for me.

Connie: Hey, *never* feel ashamed of what you don't know. If you've read *Power Your Personal Finance* and listened to episodes 211 and 341—I'll link to those in the show notes—you've heard me dish about my own background, growing up in a working class Mexican immigrant family. My parents *never* talked about money, at least not beyond worrying we never had enough! I had to learn everything all on my own.

Frank: You still grew up on—*in*—a world where money is incredibly important for just about everything, right? But the whole *concept* is just incredibly *alien* to someone like me. I'm, uh, foreign…

Connie: [*Chuckles.*] I didn't want to comment on your accent, but it is lovely.

Frank: Thanks, Ms. Padilla. But my point is that things are completely different where I'm from. 401(k)s, IRAs, HSAs, FSAs, CFPs…we don't have anything remotely like that. I can barely wrap my ten—my head around it all. [*Pause*] It's all just so —so—so *nonsensical!*

Connie: Calm down, Frank. Relax! I know *all* about feeling like a fish out of water. But honestly, you're in exactly the same boat as many of my other listeners. Possibly in an even *better* boat, because you haven't had a chance to develop bad money habits in the first place! And rest assured, I'm here to help you navigate that ship to financial freedom.

Frank: You…you really think you can help me, Ms. Padilla?

Connie: Absolutely! Now, let's start with the fundamentals…

The Frontpage Feed: Breaking News!
SUBJECT LINE: Shocker! Politicians
chuck plausible deniability (and little
green men are headed for Earth)
Top Ranked News (73,589,230 shares):
We Are Not Alone! World Leaders
Confess to Cover-Up, Tell Public to
Prepare to Welcome Extraterrestrial
Visitors

In a stunning revelation, the leaders of several nations today confirmed the accusations posted last week by the still-unidentified whistleblower.

At the historic joint press conference, the president of the United States and other heads of state verified the interception of a "message of intelligent extraterrestrial origin" nearly a decade ago. They further verified receipt of a second message just over one month ago on October 15 at 5:32 a.m. UTC; both missives have since been released to the public.

"Our interstellar neighbors tell us they have been observing humanity and want to learn more about us," Japan's prime minister summarized the message. "That is why they have sent an emissary."

Calculations based on information contained in the second message put the extraterrestrial ambassadors' arrival at mid-April.

"I don't know what our idiot leaders were thinking, not informing the public sooner so we'd all have more time to adjust to this new reality," said Dr. Abrams, director of the Space Policy Institute at the George Washington University. "Consequently, humanity has just *five months* to collectively roll out the red carpet."

Some humans, apparently, cannot wait. In reaction to thousands of extraterrestrial enthusiasts attempting to make contact through jerry-rigged transmitters, the U.N. Office for Outer Space Affairs posted an advisory warning against "making unauthorized diplomatic overtures that may confuse, if not endanger interplanetary relations."

Business and Finance News (7,723,459 shares): *'Completely Bonkers': Main Street, Wall Street Reaction Out of This World*

The U.S. Federal Reserve Board of Governors met this morning with leadership from central banks around the world. Their daunting task: stabilize an economic and financial system that is just starting to react to yesterday's revelation about an impending extraterrestrial visit.

"Too late," said Resh Agarwal, senior analyst with the London-based Centre for Fiscal Security. "Everything has already gone completely bonkers—that *is* the technical term, by the way."

"Bonkers" may indeed describe how both financial markets and consumers are responding to the news.

On Wall Street, stocks see-sawed wildly from opening to closing bell, repeating a pattern set by the Nikkei, Shanghai Composite, DAX, and FTSE earlier in the day. On Main Street, retailers reported record-setting activity, with customers fully in panic-buying mode. Sporting goods stores have resorted to rationing out survival and camping gear. The two most popular internet search terms yesterday were "hazmat suit" and "DIY tinfoil hat."

"Customers are literally preparing for the end of the world," said Whole Nine Yards store manager Tonya Reiss, speaking to a correspondent in El Paso, Texas. "They're stocking up on everything, from firearms to canned food. The shelves are empty; we've completely run out of aluminum foil and our vendors are backordered by as much as seven months."

LIBRARY: Latest   Episode. Downloading…
Power Your Personal Finance! Ranked #1 in genre. Please leave a review! *Episode transcript.*
Cue teaser, introductory music, sponsor plug

Connie: Happy Money Monday, everybody! I'm Connie Padilla, Certified Financial Planner, welcoming you to episode five-ninety-seven of the *Power Your Personal Finance!* podcast. This is where we talk about everything that can affect your pocketbook—and how you can *act* rather than *react*, to take control of *your* financial future. Control and discipline *is* what it's all about, especially during volatile times.

And speaking of volatility, *what* a week, huh? Stock markets plummeted, triggering the 'circuit breaker' fail-safe no fewer than *five times*—and taking all of our IRAs and 401(k)s along for the ride. Fortunately, things seemed to stabilize by the end of the week. But what will the coming weeks and months bring?

Listen. I know we're all shaken to the core by the confirmation we're not alone in the universe. It makes us reassess what's truly important, revisit the things we take for granted. And when it comes down to it, I know we *all* have the exact same question:

How is this going to affect my portfolio?

Should I sell? Should I pull everything from my retirement account? Should I convert all my assets into cash or commodities? Do I put it all into durable goods?

I want everyone listening to log out and step away from your investment apps. Take a deep breath. Do *not* let panic take control of your financial decisions. *You* are the one in control. Because here's the answer: Discipline. If you've been disciplined all along, you're all set! You have at least six to eight months of living expenses in cash on hand. You're diversified. You're prepared. You'll be *fine*. You can weather this storm. In fact, my special guest today happens to be an expert on weathering financial storms...

[*Fast forward.* TIME: 27:05]

We'll end the show as we always do, by reading a review left by a listener. Today's review was written by our friend, Frank! Frank says: *Ms. Padilla has become my go-to resource for everything personal finance. Since she took my question on the live show, I've joined the Power Your Personal Finance! online community, where I've been welcomed with open appendages by a group of people similarly inspired to make Ms. Padilla's 'Financial Fund-amentals' part of their daily lives. I know I still have a lot to learn, but now I feel confident that I'm well on my way. Thank you, Ms. Padilla—I'm your newest, biggest fan!*

🐰

**Power   Your   Personal   Finance!
Community   Platform.** Enter username
and password.

Hot Topic: *What IS ETs' grift, anyway?*
(2,739 replies)

Excerpt—*P.J. Kuppenheimer, an economist
once ridiculed in academic circles for his
obsession over proving the so-called Theory
of Interstellar Trade, was appointed this
week to the White House Council of
Economic Advisers. In his first interview
with the news media, Kuppenheimer
expressed skepticism over the stated
intentions of the "Ambassadors"—as the
metaverse has dubbed the extraterrestrials
—declaring, "It is entirely irrational for any
intelligent being—that is, any self-
interested, utility-maximizing individual—
to make the long and arduous interstellar
journey simply to meet another species in
person. These 'Ambassadors' clearly must
have some profit motive in mind. Our job is
to determine just what, exactly, that may
be—and how to prepare for it."* Related
link: *The Grifter's Guide to the Galaxy,*
MacroEconDaily.NET interview with P.J.

Kuppenheimer, Ph.D., Chicago School of Economics.

Moderator: Okay, folks! Before you post, remember to answer today's poll: What's the *real* motivation driving these "Ambassadors" to visit our little blue planet?
- (1) They've screwed up their own planet and want ours
- (2) They're straight-up conquerors and just want our planet period, no justification required
- (3) They've cooked up some grift that makes interstellar travel worth their while

[Tally: (1) 25%; (2) 13%; (3) 62%]

Financially Fit: Seriously? 38% of the people here must be hard-core preppers if they really believe in #1 or #2. [215 likes; 52 LOLs]

ETFrank: "Preppers"? [7 likes]

Retire Early or Bust: I agree, Financially Fit; I think the good prof's hit the nail on the head. Between time dilation and the opportunity costs, in-person interstellar travel just doesn't make sense. There has to be *something* that makes it worth their while. But what? [198 likes]

ETFrank: "Preppers?" [2 likes; 32 eye-rolls]

$$$urvivor: Their technology has to be light years ahead of ours, right? My bet's on them manufacturing a bunch of tiny gizmos super-cheap on their own planet and selling them for insane profit margins here. [278 likes, 53 shares]

ETFrank: Why would the Ambassadors want to sell anything? The message stated our entire goal is a free and open exchange of cultures and ideas! [143 likes, 27 hearts]

ETFrank: Sorry; typo. "Their" entire goal. Also, IDK "preppers." [5 LOLs]

Retire Early or Bust: Come on, ETFrank! That's the classic freemium model. They'll start out giving away their nifty toys, and just wait—soon enough, we won't be able to live without 'em. *Then* they'll be all: Surprise! It's a subscription service —and start charging us through the nose—or whatever orifice. Hook. Line. Sinker. [317 likes, 46 shares]

Moderator: Here you go, Frank: [Link to: *Neighborhood Nut Jobs or Smart Cookies? Top (legal) tips from America's premier preppers on* *setting aside enough food and ammo to last through the End of Days.*]

The Frontpage Feed: Mid-day Edition
SUBJECT LINE: *Ray guns or hostess gift? Here's how to prepare for five different First Contact scenarios*
Top Ranked News (207,403 shares): *Third Message a Charm? Ambassadors Claim Friendly Intentions*

The World Ambassador Greeting Operations Network today announced interception of a third message, as the public counts down the four months remaining until First Contact. Both earth-based and orbiting telescopes tracked the latest message's trajectory back to the extraterrestrial ship, which, according to physicists, is rapidly decelerating and anticipated to cross into the Oort Cloud by this Friday.

"The Ambassadors once again stated their goal is to establish diplomatic relations and learn about humanity," said a spokesperson with Welcome WAGON— the nickname given to the rapidly-assembled international coordinating committee charged with establishing interspecies relations.

"Taken at face value, the Ambassadors are definitely trying to stress their friendly intentions," said Dr. Ixchel Ramirez, astrobiologist with the National Autonomous University of Mexico. She and her interdisciplinary team of scientists, data analysts and linguists have scrutinized the details of every message received thus far. "The picture we've put together so far indicates a culture dedicated to both intellectual and cultural advancement, almost as imperatives to personal and societal growth."

Economist Peter Jeremiah ("P.J.") Kuppenheimer, who recently skyrocketed from obscurity to a household name, is not so inclined to take the Ambassadors at face value. "Why are the Ambassadors trying so hard to convince us of their benign motives?" he scoffed in a series of critical tweets. "Frankly, it's suspicious."

Marketing industry veteran Shahad Khoury agreed. "They're establishing their brand identity ahead of time," she theorized at a recent conference of the Euro-West Asia Advertising Alliance. "Like everyone, they're selling something—and customers prefer supporting a brand they already feel positive about."

Security experts take a more pessimistic interpretation of these messages. "It could be propaganda intended to soften us up in advance of a full-scale invasion," suggested Mai Begay, fellow at the Center for Strategic Defense, based in Arlington, Virginia.

In the meantime, Welcome WAGON has released preliminary details on the planned Landing Ceremony. A multinational site selection committee is wrapping up evaluation of candidate locations to serve as the Ambassadors' embassy.

Business and Finance News (24,869 shares): *Defense Investors Hang Ten as Sector Surfs Wave Fueled by Military Dollars; Charitable Giving and Luxury Travel Soar*

Shortly after news broke about the so-called "Ambassadors'" upcoming rendezvous with Earth, financial analysts predicted that the value of fiat currencies around the world would plunge, warning markets would experience a meltdown as people gathered with their loved ones to wait out—with dread or excitement—the impending arrival.

Instead, the revelation birthed a whole new set of momentum stocks. Despite reassurances the Ambassadors are not out for conquest, not everyone on Wall Street—or in Washington, Beijing, Riyadh or Moscow— is banking on a kumbaya First Contact. Defense contractors, firearm manufacturers, and distributors of survival gear are all driving a robust bull market after an initial dip.

At the same time, megachurches and community organizations find themselves overwhelmed by donations. "People are desperate to redeem their souls before the 'invasion'," observed Jenny Zhou, pastor with the First Lutheran Church of Kalamazoo, Michigan.

Tourism and recreation are also benefitting. The industry reported a 300 percent increase in spending compared to this time last year, with consumers throwing their retirement savings at "bucket list" items. "Nobody's even raising an eyebrow at the waiver form these days," said Sergio Martinez, owner and CEO of St. Croix-based X-Treme Ocean Skydiving, LLP. "They just shrug and say, 'Why the hell not?'"

@ConniePadillaPYPF | Power   Your
Personal   Finance®
@PYPersonalFinancePodcast • Jan 14
837.5K Followers

Wow!   Incredibly   honored   to   be
recognized as a "top finance expert" by
@PersonalInvestorMag this week.

> [link to *Personal Investor Magazine*.
> Where are Americans Turning for
> Financial Advice During the
> Impending Apocalypse?]
> [2.7K replies, 5.3K retweets, 8.6K
> likes]

@ConniePadillaPYPF | Power   Your
Personal   Finance®
@PYPersonalFinancePodcast • Jan 16
859.6K Followers

Had a great chat this week with my
fellow   money   guru   @TKRawlins   on
@TheTalkExchange   about   all   the
#marketcraziness right now.

> [link to *Wall Street Bytes*.
> Technology Stocks Tumble Across
> the Motherboard: NASDAQ stumbles

as industry doomsayers claim technologically advanced "Ambassadors" could spell the end for Silicon Valley.]

@ConniePadillaPYPF | Power Your Personal Finance® @PYPersonalFinancePodcast • Jan 16 859.6K Followers

But let's talk about what's happening on #MainStreet! Next week on the podcast I'll do a deep dive into how the Ambassadors are affecting the pocketbooks of REAL PEOPLE. DM me if you have a story you'd like to share!

[1.7K replies, 5.8K retweets, 10.4K likes]

Message to ConniePadillaPYPF from ETFrank1701 • Jan 23

Hi, Ms. Padilla. You probably don't remember me, but I was caller 7 on Power Your Personal Finance live stream episode #10. You even told me to reach out anytime if I still had trouble taking control of my personal finance journey.

Your words of empowerment that day really inspired me. So much so that I'm now the de facto "economics expert" among my friends and coworkers—they've even started asking ME for advice! Whenever I'm unsure of the answer, I'll reread a chapter of your book, replay one of your podcast episodes, or ask the PYPF community for help.

But now we all have the same question on our minds, and it's one I just don't know how to answer: Why in the universe is humanity reacting the way it is to the Ambassadors' arrival?

We just don't get it. I mean, the Ambassadors were really clear on having peaceful intentions. Officially, world leaders keep saying this is great news for the planet. But you—Connie Padilla, #1 personal finance guru—always say that money speaks louder than words. Well, a lot of people are spending money in ways that show they're scared of an invasion or think the Ambassadors are out to cheat everybody.

So, can you tell me: WHY are humans reacting this way? And what do YOU think about it?

Thanks so much; loved the last episode!

Frank

P.S. Which "rational, intelligent being" came up with the invasion scenario, anyway? It makes NO sense for an invader to give their invadee a heads-up IMHO.

Message to ETFrank1701 from ConniePadillaPYPF • Feb 12

Hey, Frank!

So sorry for the delay—I was COMPLETELY overwhelmed by all the terrific personal finance stories folks sent me last month. Teach me to ask half the metaverse to DM me. :(But of course, I remember my newest, biggest fan! I even told you to reach out to me anytime, right?

It's super interesting you and your friends are putting yourself in the Ambassadors' shoes (do they even have shoes? LOL). Because I'd say the issue here is that the rest of humanity is NOT putting itself in the Ambassadors' shoes; nope, not at all!

It's our first time meeting extraterrestrials—so who or what else do we even have to compare them to, besides ourselves? FWIW, I'd say most people assume the Ambassadors are a lot like us and weighing the risks vs. rewards of First Contact based on that. Those "peaceful intentions," the promises of cultural exchange, whatever goods & services they (probably) have to sell? They just don't outweigh the risk of an invasion (and don't even think of bringing logic into the conversation, my friend) or—more likely— being rolled by little green men.

Again, GREAT question, and maybe one I'll post a video about later in the week!

Connie

Message to ConniePadillaPYPF from ETFrank1701 • Feb 13

Hi, Ms. Padilla.

Well, that's SUPER depressing.

I mean, if you were the Ambassadors, how could you even counter that?

And do YOU feel that way, too? Or are you just another person trying to make a buck off the situation? I'm such a fan of yours, but I have to admit I'm also kind of disappointed in you right now. You're racking up all the ratings, giving people all the advice on 'weathering the storm' and 'profiting from the uncertainty'. But are you thinking AT ALL about what this'll mean for the future of humanity when the Ambassadors see what's happening and decide WTH and go home? It's risk vs. reward, after all! What's the reward for the

Ambassadors if humanity won't even give them a real chance?

In the end, nobody gains, and everyone loses.

Frank

Message to ConniePadillaPYPF from ETFrank1701 • Feb 14

Hi, Ms. Padilla.

First off, I'm really sorry. I was a jerk in my last message and I wouldn't blame you for blocking me altogether.

But if you haven't, can I admit I really was hoping you had the answer, just like you always seem to have the answer in all your books and podcasts. I have to confess I'm personally invested in this (no pun intended), though I can't say much more.

Most of the time, I agree with my colleagues: the Ambassadors SHOULD leave if this is going to be the reception. We'd like to believe humanity has a lot of potential, even with all the evil they do to each other and their planet. But, with this? Unlike humans, Ambassadors aren't going to throw good money after bad, and there really seems to be no hope, at least not for both our peoples coming together. And yet—I can't help recalling that there really IS potential. And I realize: both of us DO have a lot to gain. Not $$$, but a lot to learn, to share, to explore together. Both of us winners.

If you're right, like you usually are, and it's all about risk vs. reward, maybe the real question is: How do we go about changing the balance?

I know it's a big ask of one personal finance guru. But you're always telling people to find their own power. Well, YOU have a lot of power—all the followers and admirers who've been inspired by you. I just wish you'd use it for something much bigger than selling books or advising people on their 401(k)s.

Still your biggest fan,
Frank

The Frontpage Feed: Special Edition
SUBJECT LINE: ***Has First Contact been cancelled?!***
Top Ranked News (49,076,329 shares): ***Ambassadors' Ship No Longer on Course to Rendezvous with Earth***

Political leaders and science fiction afficionados around the world panicked yesterday morning when several Earth-based and orbiting observatories, which have kept their instruments trained on the incoming vessel for months, all reported a sudden change in the trajectory at around seven o'clock UTC. Welcome WAGON released an official statement at two o'clock in the afternoon, confirming the reports but cautioning the public not to jump to conclusions.

"We are all puzzled and, yes, concerned about this reported change in the ship's flight path. But rest assured we have our top astrophysicists looking into it," the statement declared. "We must remember that the Ambassadors are, technologically speaking, leaps and bounds ahead of us. For all we know, this anomaly may be well within expected parameters."

"Maybe they forgot something?" was the top punchline on the late-night comedy shows. Similar humorous memes quickly gained popularity across the metaverse.

But others fail to see the new development as a joking matter. The now-vindicated whistleblower, credited with starting the entire chain of events, returned yesterday afternoon to the virtual public square, claiming yet another message from the Ambassadors was intercepted and held back from public release. "Even I'm not certain what, exactly, is in that message," the former insider admitted. "But it sure as heck sent everyone into a tizzy." The White House press secretary immediately denied the claim, as have spokespeople with the other nations cited in the allegation.

Welcome WAGON in the meantime has convened an emergency session, set to meet tomorrow morning.

Stay tuned for more reporting from *The Frontpage Feed* as this story continues to develop.

Business and Finance News (10,492 shares): *Closing Bell Round-up*

Personal finance juggernaut Connie Padilla this week announced an undetermined hiatus of her popular podcast, *Power Your Personal Finance!* along with a pause on all future interviews and speaking engagements. She gave no reason, only telling her millions of fans through social media to "Stay tuned: something big is on its way!"

Speculation immediately arose that Ms. Padilla is using this time to launch a new Power Your Personal Finance branded initiative. The personal finance guru's popularity shot through the stratosphere as the Ambassadors' ship drew closer to Earth, attracting an increasing number of fans and admirers with her trademark calm and steady advice. "Connie really has her finger on the pulse of Main Street," said T.K. Rawlins, who often appears with Ms. Padilla on shows like The Talk Exchange and Financial Forecast. "It's no wonder she's so quickly become not just America's, but *everyone's* personal finance confidant."

Indeed, only White House Economic Adviser P.J. Kuppenheimer has similar name recognition, "but without the comfort factor," according to Rawlins. "I trust her," commented a member of the *Power Your Personal Finance!* Community Platform, who posts by the name of "$$ $urvivor." "Connie really gets me, gets *us*," gushed Retire Early or Bust, another member of the online community. "Whatever she has in store, I know it'll be huge!"

Message to ConniePadillaPYPF from ETFrank1701 • Feb 20
　　Hi, Ms. Padilla.

I hope you're doing well. Since I never heard back from you, I guess you must be very busy. Or you really did block me, after all.

This is the last time I'll contact you, and it's to say goodbye. My job transfer's been cancelled, so there's no longer any reason to continue on with my personal finance education. I will miss all your advice and inspiration. I learned so much from you, not only about personal finance and economics, but gained a better understanding of the world in general.

On a final note, I read you've taken a step back from your media empire to focus on "something big". I can only hope my last message inspired you in some small way, though nothing like how much you've inspired me. Either way, I wish you and everyone in the PYPF community only the very best.

Frank

Message to ETFrank1701 from ConniePadillaPYPF • Feb 21

Hey, Frank!

You should have a little more faith in me, if you really are my biggest fan! Didn't I say I could help you?

I wasn't offended at all by your message, though I was pretty stunned. Yours was the biggest challenge ANYONE has ever offered me—and probably the most meaningful, too. It made all the advice I've been called on to give up to then seem small and petty in comparison.

BTW, do you know why I started giving personal finance advice in the first place? Coming from a family with very little, I saw how money gives people so many more choices. Funny; now I see it works the other way around, too—obsessing over wealth can really limit us, huh? Your words pushed me to see things from another perspective. Through "alien eyes," LOL.

You're 100% right about all of it. We would all lose out if our two peoples never met and learned from each other. You're also right that I do have a lot of influence, more than I realized. So now I'm planning to use that power for "something big." Something much, much bigger than selling books or advising people on their 401(k)s.

I'm going to change that balance.

Connie

Message   to   ETFrank1701   from
ConniePadillaPYPF • Feb 21

Y'know, thinking back, I never actually
gave you my personal mail, hmm?

Tell your friends and coworkers you'll
be moving forward with that "transfer,"
after all.

***Power   Your   Personal   Finance!*
Community Platform.** Enter username
and password.

Hot Topic: Discuss Connie Padilla's latest
article in *Personal Investor!* (3,228 replies)

Excerpt—*If you have an entrepreneurial
streak, arrival of the "Ambassadors" could
mean an opportunity to finally kick off that
side-hustle. Think about it: an entirely
different species could open up whole new
markets for goods and services. Instead of*
reacting *to First Contact, be* proactive *and
brainstorm ways to pivot and boost your
earnings potential.* Related link: *The Smart
Side-Hustle*, available at the following
retailers.

Moderator: Way to go, Connie! Okay,
folks: let's get *proactive* in this
forum. Share some of *your* ideas for
Post-First Contact side hustles!

Retire Early or Bust: Do these aliens even breathe our air? My brother-in-law works for a factory that makes oxygen for hospitals. Maybe we could manufacture whatever *they* breathe and sell it? [37 likes]

Country Mouse Investing in Cheese: I'll bet even my rat-hole hick town would seem exotic to visitors from another world. I could start a tour guide gig! "Come and see Earth's biggest ball of twine..." [11 hearts]

Mortgage Burning Party: Not a bad idea, CMIIC! Personally, I think souvenirs are where it's at. I'll call my company "Made on Earth". [52 likes]

[*jump to latest comments*]

Feeling Bearish: Hold on here, people. Who says the Ambassadors will cough up cash for anything? Maybe they don't even have anything like "money" where they're from. Honestly, I think our girl Connie is being too optimistic this time. [5 likes]

Retire Early or Bust: Maybe Connie IS being an optimist—but isn't she right that nothing positive will happen until you start being proactive and take power? And isn't that better than throwing trillions of dollars at tanks and aircraft and crap that probably wouldn't last half a minute against a bunch of space invaders? [542 likes]

Country Mouse Investing in Cheese: Hey, I say it's worth taking the risk! *This* mouse is grabbing the chance to get out of the corporate rat race. [73 likes]

Mortgage Burning Party: Does that mean the Ambassadors will buy my souvenirs? [37 likes]

The Frontpage Feed:
SUBJECT LINE: *First Contact back on track and straight to the bank!*
Top Ranked News (43, 722, 549 shares): *'Just a Blip': Ambassadors Stay the Course for Little Blue Planet*

The world held its breath last week when it appeared the Ambassadors had aborted their mission. 'We all just about sullied our pants,' relayed a member of Welcome WAGON, on condition of anonymity. "Considering all the time, effort and money put into preparing for First Contact—*the* event of the millennium

—what would we even *do* if the Ambassadors decided to change their minds?!"

The shock turned into relief this Tuesday, when observatories confirmed the Ambassadors were still making their way to Earth, albeit slightly behind schedule. "It must have been just a blip," chuckled Lesedi Nkosi, astrophysicist at the South African National Space Agency. "I guess Welcome WAGON shouldn't roll up the red carpet just yet."

Many are now criticizing the whistleblower for inciting unnecessary panic with allegations about the cover up of a fourth message, received from the Ambassadors at the same time their ship appeared to veer off course. "My fellow world leaders and I are committed to open and honest dialogue with the public about every aspect of this momentous development in human history," the United States president spoke yesterday evening from the Oval Office. "The time for secrecy and self-interest has passed."

Business and Finance News (132,837 shares): *Will Extraterrestrials Put Extra Cash in Our Pockets? This Personal Finance Guru Thinks So.*

What started as a provocative article in *Personal Investor* is now all every wannabe entrepreneur is talking about.

Connie Padilla—of *Power Your Personal Finance!* fame—set off a global conversation last week with a powerful essay [click here] laying out her argument that the Ambassadors' arrival will stimulate innovation and goose the economy. " 'Ambassadors' is a misnomer," Ms. Padilla proclaimed. "Replace 'alien' and 'extraterrestrial' with 'customer' and 'client.' You want to approach First Contact like a *real* entrepreneur? Take control of the situation. Chuck that tinfoil hat, put away your H.G. Wells, and start drafting your goddamn business plan, already!"

Padilla's messages of financial empowerment garnered her a loyal fan base that ballooned with the first revelations about the Ambassadors. Economists around the world are finally starting to take her seriously, too. "Ms. Padilla may have a point," allowed P.J. Kuppenheimer, the White House economic adviser who has been openly skeptical about the Ambassadors' intentions. "Under the Theory of Interstellar Trade, and despite the obvious challenges related to transport costs, the Ambassadors could be incentivized to manufacture high-value goods and invest their profits locally. That would be to Earth's economic advantage."

The financial markets appear to agree with both Padilla and Kuppenheimer. Blue chip stocks rallied again, but this time the action on Wall Street wasn't concentrated in the defense sector. Investors across the board are expressing renewed optimism over the future. One manufacturer after another has announced hefty investments in R&D in anticipation of the Ambassadors' arrival. The effects aren't limited to the big corporate players, either; state and local agencies reported a surge in the pulling of new business licenses and filing of articles of incorporation.

"It's time to stop being scared," Padilla encouraged members of her online community platform. "Be excited!"

Message to ConniePadillaPYPF from ETFrank1701 • Mar 18

Hi, Ms. Padilla,

I meant to message you earlier, but things have been incredibly hectic, with everyone making final preparations to open up our new location. That's right: my transfer is on course to happen after all! It may sound odd, but it's really all thanks to you. The only downside is that things are busier than ever as a result, but I'm not complaining!

I know you've been extremely busy, too. I think every other communication beamed from Earth these days has your signature on it. You seem to be everywhere—in articles, on your podcast, popping into your community forum, giving interviews, bringing people together. I'm amazed by all you're doing, inspiring people to see not just the risks, but all the rewards a relationship between our peoples could bring.

Most of all, I'm amazed that someone like me could inspire someone like you. You were right all along, too: it's up to each of us to take power over our own future—and that includes our shared future. It's a future I'm feeling so much more optimistic about, too.

Your biggest fan in the universe,
Frank

The Frontpage Feed: Special Edition

SUBJECT LINE: *Get ready for the biggest watch party ever: ten celebrity chefs share their out-of-this-world recipes*

Top Ranked News (4,043,852 shares): *'We're On Our Way!' Ambassadors Reassure Humanity*

Relief, joy, and anticipation were on clear display around the world with the public release of the Ambassadors' latest missive to Earth. According to the Welcome WAGON Secretariat, the message amounts to confirmation of arrival and an apology for "potentially causing confusion" among human officials due to "a mild correction in trajectory".

"We remain enthusiastic about this first meeting between our respective species," the Ambassadors emphasized in multiple languages. "And we hope this is just the beginning of new opportunities for our two peoples. We both have much to exchange, and countless ways to profit from diplomatic ties."

Business and Finance News (98,302 shares): *Ambassadors' Latest Message Sends Markets Soaring*

"We both have much to exchange, and countless ways to profit," was the sentence from the Ambassador's latest missive that investors zoomed in on.

"Are they talking trade deals?" said Yan Sundström, Director-General of the World Trade Organization, now undergoing drastic restructuring in preparation for the Ambassadors' arrival. "What items will be on the table?"

Welcome WAGON, apparently taking personal finance guru Connie Padilla's advice to "take control of the situation," announced formation of an international blue-ribbon panel to analyze the economic opportunities presented by establishing trade relations with extraterrestrials. The panel, to be co-chaired by Ms. Padilla herself, along with White House Economic Adviser P.J. Kuppenheimer, will report out a framework set of recommendations prior to First Contact.

When asked at the press conference about her outsize impact, driving this new wave of optimism, Padilla replied: "I don't believe that one person alone, no matter how influential, can move the entire world. But, as my biggest fan in the universe recently reminded me, I can—and I should—give it a nudge."

The Nikkei reached an all-time high today on the news, with the FTSE closing just a whisker below its own record.

Message to ETFrank1701 from ConniePadillaPYPF • Mar 19

Hey, Frank!

That's fantastic news!!

I guess my diabolical plan worked, after all. What's the point of having power and influence if you can't use it to make the galaxy a better place? Though I guess I should feel a little bit bad about it; in a way, I'm tricking people about how everyone is going to "profit" from First Contact. But I'm not wrong about that in a bigger sense: everyone WILL profit from our peoples meeting, just not in the way they're assuming I meant.

While you're making your big move, I'm thinking about my next step, too. I want humanity to have some grander ambition to aspire to than just feathering our own nest. Sure, maybe we need to use the promise of wealth as a goad in the short run, but long-term I want us to look up toward the stars instead of always down at our own pocketbooks. I've never considered taking on something so huge, but maybe if we work together, it'll be easier to tackle? I think we make a "stellar" team, LOL.

So—now that your transfer's on again, I think we should finally meet in person. In, say, two months, four days, eleven hours and change from when I hit "send"?

Connie

Message   to   ETFrank1701   from ConniePadillaPYPF • Mar 19

I also think it's about time you knock off this "Ms. Padilla" stuff and start calling me "Connie".

Message   to   ETFrank1701   from ConniePadillaPYPF • Mar 19

What should I call you?

The Frontpage Feed: Morning Edition
SUBJECT LINE: *WELCOME TO EARTH!*
Top Ranked News (102,486,093 shares):
Ambassadors   Arrive: A Photojournalist's   Moment-by-Moment Diary

Caption 1: "Houston, they've arrived." *View from International Space Station.*

Ambassador mothership parks in Earth orbit. *Caption 2:* "Bienvenidos!" *Montevideo, Uruguay.* Ambassador landing craft touches down in the middle of Plaza Independencia. *Caption 3:* "A historic meeting." *Foreground:* Ambassador delegation exchanges greetings with Welcome WAGON emissaries. *Caption 4.* "We have much to learn from each other." *New York City, United States.* Ambassador Glolteesh Hroné, left, delivers speech before United Nations General Assembly.

Business and Finance News (59,340,271 shares): *Ambassadoronomics 101 To Precede Trade Talks*

Markets soared Tuesday on affirmation the Ambassadors are, indeed, eager to open trade discussions with the World Trade Organization—the first time that body will truly represent the entire planet. "We're going to make the 'Made on Earth' label *mean* something," Yan Sundström proclaimed at yesterday's press conference, the Ambassadors' Special Attaché for Interspecies Business and Finance, Flelviing Rlankonī, at his side.

Investor optimism remained undampened despite both parties citing a need for preliminary discussions before trade talks begin in earnest. "We're not even talking about an apples-to-oranges comparison in how our two economies work. Hell, we're not even talking fruit," said U.S. Trade Representative Marcela Tsai. "The Ambassadors operate in a completely different manner, and it's going to take some time just to wrap our heads around it."

"The Ambassadors seem to take the concept of 'knowledge economy' to an entirely new level—one apparently based on an open sharing mechanism rather than the exchange-for-value economic models we're familiar with on Earth," explained Claire Ahaisse, economic sociologist with Princeton University. "If their claims are accurate, life on the Ambassadors' home world blows every single metric of our own Legatum Prosperity Index out of the water when it comes to measuring global well-being," she went on to add. "Personally, I'd love to know how they do it."

Ahaisse joins a growing multitude of economists, sociologists, political scientists, philosophers, and civic activists around the world fascinated by what humanity is learning about the Ambassadors. "At the same time we're selling the Ambassadors on human goods and services, scholars and the mainstream public alike are increasingly 'sold' on what they have to offer us," Ahaisse noted.

To lay the foundation for negotiations, the WTO's Blue-Ribbon Panel on Exploring Interstellar Economic Opportunity is launching a series of cross-cultural learning sessions; special attaché Rlankoní will be representing the Ambassadors in these conversations. The events will be open to the public and simulcast around the globe.

Early reports of close collaboration between the special attaché and the panel's chair, Connie Padilla, are particularly promising. "Connie and Flelviing hit it off right away," observed Ms. Padilla's co-chair, T.J. Kuppenheimer. "They make a pretty stellar team."

LIBRARY: **Latest**   **Episode.** Downloading...
Power Your Personal Finance! Ranked #1 in genre. Please leave a review! *Episode transcript.*

Cue teaser, introductory music, sponsor plug

Connie: Happy   spread-the-wealth Wednesday, everybody! I'm Connie Padilla, Certified Financial Planner, welcoming you to episode seven-eighty-seven of the *Power Your Personal Finance!* podcast. Where we talk not just about everything that can affect your pocketbook—but also peel back the rules and assumptions governing the game *all* of us have been playing. It's been gratifying, hearing from so many listeners how much you appreciate the new direction this show has taken these past few months.

Which is why the *Power Your Personal Finance!* network is launching an entirely *new* show all about exploring the new financial frontiers First Contact has opened for us. Can you believe it's been over a *year* now? Anyhow, it's about time we really explore the potential of this still-nascent relationship between our species.

Most exciting of all, I'll be co-hosting the show with my best buddy, Flelviing Rlankoni! Truly an extraordinary personality—explorer, academic, diplomat. And, I would say, something of an entrepreneur himself, though he'd probably disagree! Flelviing's made a study of human culture, specializing in economics and finance, and never fails to surprise with his insights.

Anyhow, this show will be looking at the big picture, aimed at listeners from both planets. We'll talk about how to invest in *super* foreign markets, the nuts and bolts of building cross-species enterprises, pros and cons of doing business across the light years, and how to survive life on a predominantly capitalist planet—plus successful alternatives elsewhere and lessons we've all learned along the way.

And every episode we'll ask of humans and Ambassadors alike: how can we improve?

That's why we're calling it *Outperforming Ourselves*.

And to give you a little taste of what's to come, I've brought Flelviing on as my surprise guest for today's show! Oh, and don't be surprised if I seem to slip up on his name every now and again—kind of an inside joke.

Now, before we start, a quick disclaimer. You know the boilerplate, folks. *Power Your Personal Finance* is purely for educational and entertainment purposes. Anything said on this show should not be construed as individual financial, legal, tax, or accounting advice; listeners are advised to discuss their personal financial situation and goals with a financial professional. And remember: while we talk about stocks, bonds, and interstellar investments on this show, past performance is *not* indicative of future results!

Let's all aim to do better.

See C.H. Rosenberg's story "Indicative of Future Results" online at Metaphorosis.
If you liked it, leave a comment. Authors love that!
Remember to subscribe to our e-mail updates so you'll know when new stories are posted.

About the story

This story originates with my realization that the modern-day and increasingly digital personal finance community—and especially the Financial Independence Retire Early (FIRE) movement—is one worthy of intensive anthropological study. After all, doesn't it have all the elements of a modern-day cult? It has its own prophets and evangelists, its peculiar vernacular, its sacred and beloved texts, an undeniable emphasis on self-help and personal growth, all of it resting on those irrepressible American values: Grit! Determination! Self-reliance! At the same time this swelling movement delivers benefits in the form of sound financial guidance, this advice rarely makes it to the eyes and ears of those outside the already privileged strata of society. Woven through all the podcasts, videos, blogs, and plethora of digital content is a thread of toxicity, where social safety nets are scorned and the poor blatantly blamed for their poverty. With this in mind, I watched with the rest of the world as first the Great Recession and more recently the COVID-19 pandemic revealed a spiderweb of fractures in our existing financial and economic system. Both are fascinating case studies into how many will find opportunities in any situation, whether for ill—such as grifters and demagogues—or for good—such as through entrepreneurial and charitable endeavors. I wondered what a true outside observer—an extraterrestrial anthropologist, as it were—would think of all this. Shocked? Horrified? Impressed? Would that observer see the humor in the situation? Would that observer have another point view and—

more importantly—be willing to share it? I've always loved First Contact stories for this reason: they represent an opportunity to reassess humanity from a new perspective at the same time they represent a fresh start.

A question for the author

Q: What is the scariest or most disturbing story you've ever read?

A: The most disturbing stories I read are ostensibly nonfiction, especially the narratives written to justify the unconscionable. Examples include the Requirimiento, asserting Spain's authority over (read: invasion of) the Americas and often read—in Latin—to Indigenous peoples without any interpreter or even delivered to an empty beach, or Chief Judge Marshall's justification in *Johnson v. M'Intosh* that "Conquest gives a title which the Courts of the conqueror cannot deny".

About the author

Writing as an armchair economist, in real life C.H. Rosenberg is a grizzled policy wonk who spent an early career fighting in the trenches of local politics in Southern California. Rosenberg currently works at one of Washington, D.C.'s many alphabet-soup think tanks, brainstorming all sorts of amazing ways to save the planet.

Medusa Rising

Christine Lucas

Long ago, it was scholars and archaeologists who came knocking on Lengo's door, asking permission to go search her land for antiquities. Then, after her late grandson Nikolas did what he did, came the police officers and the media vultures. Tonight, it's one of the fascist scum her Nikolas befriended in Athens, where she shipped him off twenty years ago to get an education. And what did that air-headed boy of hers do? He joined a cult—or, rather, a gang? Whatever their ilk, one of them just knocked on her door hours after dusk, expecting to be invited in.

"Evening, ma'am. I'm Jason, a friend of your late grandson's." He slides his gloved palm between her creaky door and the doorframe, so she can't shut it in his face. "I just sailed in from Piraeus for Nikos' *saranta*. Can I come in?"

Countless little voices in Lengo's mind warn her against inviting the evil in, including the whisper of her late grandma, who's sitting on her usual spot by the stove, knitting with ethereal thread and needles. Still, Lengo finds it hard to turn away anyone, especially in stormy weather. She has never turned away a visitor. But now times have changed. Jason's kind has resurfaced, and they're loud and violent. She'd rather avoid an altercation with someone twice her size. But perhaps she shouldn't judge him from how he carries himself? Perhaps there's good in him, still. After all, he did remember Nikolas' memorial service. The funerals of perpetrators of murder/suicide are lonely events, their forty-days memorial services even more so. There should be someone—even *this* one—to pay respects to her boy who took the wrong path and lost his way.

So she lets him in.

He wipes his combat boots on her worn mat, bows his shaven head to cross the narrow doorframe, and shoves his gloves in the pockets of his camouflage pants. He scowls at her low-roofed two-room home—the other parts of her once-spacious residence have long succumbed to the storms of the Aegean Sea, and no longer keep the winter chill out. He frowns at the pitiful fire in the hearth and the badly-aged covers on the worn divan that doubles as her bed. One glance at his combat boots, and the cat bolts out of the window, seeking better company in the night. Lengo's yaya's ghost wraps up her spectral knitting and follows the cat.

Jason wrinkles his nose at the smells from her stove and her dinner table—reheated lentil soup and yesterday's bread, with a side of olives and a glass of cheap retsina wine. But he draws a chair and plops himself at the table, expecting to be served.

Well, then.

Lengo reaches into the second pot on her stove and serves him the leftovers of a dish with rice and chicken. She's saved that for after the memorial service tomorrow, and almost regrets wasting this dish on the likes of him, but it might be worth it just to see the look on his face. He digs in, helping it down with chunks of stale bread and gulps of retsina. Between mouthfuls, he manages a compliment.

"That's some damn-good pilaf, Kera-Lengo!"

"Thank you." She sits across him, her back rigid, and clasps her hands on her apron.

"Family recipe?"

"You could say that. From my grandaughter-in law's side; her grandma taught her how to make it, back in Mogadishu, and Astur taught me. It's called *bariis iskukaris*, and I hear it's a very popular Somali dish."

He stops chewing mid-mouthful at the mention of Nikolas' late wife. His hands freeze while breaking bread in chunks. Lengo holds her breath and wonders if he'll spit it out.

He doesn't. Instead, he swallows and resumes manhandling the bread, spreading crumbs all over her white table cloth that has seen happier times and much better guests.

"Well." He shovels more spiced rice into his mouth. "Her kind does have *some* skill with cooking." Another mouthful of wine, and his face mellows a little. "It reminds me of a dish my late yaya used to make, from Constantinople. I miss her cooking."

Several questions crowd at the tip of Lengo's tongue: Which 'kind' would that be? Somali women? Black women? Or women in general? And should she clock him with her trusted cast-iron pan? At least his grandma isn't around anymore to see what he's become.

But she's mopped up enough blood already, after Nikolas did what he did to Astur, and she's tired. She'd rather not deal with more police questions. The bigoted idiot will eat and snore and attend the service tomorrow, then get the hell out of her home, and back to his dungeon or wherever his kind gather in Athens. So she squeezes her hands onto her apron until her nails dig into her palms, and maintains an icy half-smile. But doubt slithers into her heart like drafts find their way into her home. Did she make a mistake letting him in?

She unlocks Nikolas' chamber for the night. Her heart flutters when she crosses the threshold, fetching fresh linen and blankets for the bed. She hasn't set one foot inside after the officers wrapped up their investigation and she got on her hands and knees cleansing the place. Can blood be ever truly cleansed, or will its echoes haunt the years to come, until the very bricks and beams crumble to pebbles and kindling?

He follows her inside, his gaze seeking the beam overhead where the noose was tied, as if expecting to see marks on the wood. Then he studies the now-bare walls. Did he really expect to see all those despicable photographs, posters, and mementos Nikolas brought back home from his time in Athens? Nikolas kept them hidden at first, but they slowly slithered into her home and their life here. Especially those photographs in which he posed with some others with similar ideology with their arms raised. They called that hail 'an ancient Greek salute', and they could all kiss her cat's ass. She knew exactly what kind of salute it was, and what that crooked cross and equally crooked meander symbol stood for. Off into the fire they went, once the police gathered all they needed from the room. The only remaining picture is a photo of Nikolas' wedding in the town's courthouse with Astur absolutely radiant beside him. Next to it, Lengo has placed an icon of the sad-eyed Virgin cradling the Infant.

Jason drops his backpack on the floor by the door and sits at the edge of the bed to untie his boots. He's comfortable in his late friend's room, as though he belongs here—as though he's family. But he's not. Lengo knows little about him, and she doesn't care to know more. The bed creaks under his weight, and Lengo's heart clenches to see *this* stranger on her grandson's bed. Astur should be there, instead of him, nursing her infant daughter, Lengo's great-grandchild. Lengo pretends to wipe her already clean hands on the apron, so he won't notice her white-knuckled fists. He doesn't notice—to him she's probably just another barely-literate old widow, grief-stricken and clad in the clothes of past decades. Her black garments and head-scarves have never been fashionable, only practical, the *uniform* of crones of the Greek countryside.

"If you need anything during the night, I'm just behind that wall," she says, and shuts the door behind her.

She huddles on the divan, wrapped in thin blankets that do little against the chill, and cries herself to sleep.

Dawn can't come fast enough.

Lengo starts from her sleep in the small hours of the night with her heart racing. She thought she heard glass shattering—what did that useless cat break this time? Has her yaya's ghost returned to torment Jason in his sleep? Or was it an infant crying? She thinks she hears the cry of a baby too often these days, the wailing a distant echo just behind her ears—an infant that cries to come home. Nikolas' spirit, that won't depart for the afterlife until after his saranta, or Astur's little girl, crying for her yaya to come and get her and bring her home?

She sits up and rubs her swollen eyes. Somewhere, window shutters bang against the wall at the north wind that whips their shores for another night. All windows are shut and bolted here; where in the Virgin's name have they become undone at this hour? She puts on her thin robe and her slippers. There's light coming from under the door to Nikolas' room—Jason should still be up, so she might as well check there first.

The room is empty. The light comes from the laptop he's left open on the desk.

The bed hasn't been slept in, and the backpack is gone. Jason left through the open window, it seems, and broke the glass doing so. But why did he slip out like a thief in the night?

She knows she shouldn't snoop on guests under her roof, but Jason is one of *them*; she owes him nothing. So Lengo leans over to check the screen on his laptop—he probably saw her long-out-dated flip phone and thought her another technologically illiterate old-timer. He didn't even bother to password-protect his laptop. His background image shows him in camouflage clothes, with a dog at his side, which looks up at him with clear adoration. She hopes that's a good sign; perhaps she misunderstood him after all, if an innocent soul trusts him. She browses through his web history, and finds exactly what she originally expected: rants and manifestos over Nation and Culture, and against everything his ilk deems beneath them: refugees, people of color, women, and all the *others* who don't rise up to their abominable standards of "true" humans.

But barely a mention of *old* women. Her skin color and her origin made her dear Astur *other* to *them*, but Lengo is nothing. *Nobody.*

Outis.

Hah. But this *Nobody* knows things. The school teacher she was before she became a wife and a mother chuckles. There's a lesson somewhere in there. But she wouldn't know where to start teaching it to Jason and the others like him. Thick-headed, thick-hearted, ignorant of the power crones hold in these parts—power held since long before the Trinity and the Twelve. It's a shame, really, the teacher inside her insists. His writing is so eloquent, so articulate and refined, and yet so vile at the same time. It shows a deep thirst for learning, and yet all the knowledge and intellect that shine through his words are twisted into weapons for his perceived war.

She sighs, and her fingers move to turn the device off, when her gaze falls onto a communication folder with her grandson's name on it. Her hand trembles mid-air. She should ignore it. It can hold only heartbreak. Hasn't her heart bled enough? Parents shouldn't live long enough to see their children die, grandparents more so. But perhaps this is part of her penance for failing her grandson.

So she opens the file. It holds both heartbreak and insight into her grandson's actions. During the investigation of the murder/suicide, the coroner and the officers discussed motives, their main focus Nikolas' past trauma from out-living his parents, and the fact he stopped his medication a month before the incident. They never told Lengo their conclusions. Small island, small community, big case that could harm tourism for the coming summer. In the end, with no perpetrator to prosecute, they wrapped up the case and moved on. The victim was just another immigrant to them, that *nobody* would miss. And tonight, *this* Nobody finds the emails that they conveniently missed, and they are dipped in poison.

Nikolas loved his wife; Lengo knows as much. He left his former 'friends' behind for Astur, and returned to the island of his forefathers to raise a family with her. But now she sees that communication with his 'friends' continued, week after week, month after month—messages accusing him of treason and desertion, oozing hatred for a girl who'd fled war and famine for a better future. *Stop those pills*, they urged him. *It's poison, clouding your vision and limiting your true potential.* It didn't take long until Nikolas' replies shifted from meek excuses and apologies to deranged rants, of how he thought that his wife stepped out in the middle of the night to copulate with monsters, and of how he feared the child that grew in her womb. Jason only fed Nikolas' delusions, urging him to leave and come back to them. To *him*, his only real friend.

The last message in the file, from Jason to Nikolas, is five words in all; five blood-chilling words:

"You know what to do."

Lengo slams the laptop shut, choking on a sob. If her body trembled a little less, she'd smash the device against the white-washed wall. She jumps to her feet to get out of there, out, to the lashing wind to cleanse her thoughts, and she stumbles on Jason's backpack. He'd shoved it under the bed, but her foot gets caught on its strap. Some of its contents spill out—a stack of papers. As her eyes adjust to the gloom now that the laptop is closed, she picks them up and sinks deeper into rage.

Some of the papers have drawings, others are print-outs, but all show similar features of a bare-chested woman—sometimes with Caucasian features, but mostly of African descent. Some resemble the frescoes of ancient Minoan ladies, but most of them depict a monstrous face over a voluptuous body, with a wild mane of serpents for hair. The last few drawings show someone in hoplite's armor cutting off the creature's head. Interesting how this monster-slaying hero's features resemble Jason's.

Lengo's heart dives for her feet. It's her fault, isn't it? She raised her Nikolas with the tales of the heroes of old—Herakles and Theseus, Perseus and Achilles. All of them great men slaying enemies and monsters. But she failed to teach him how, in real life, it's not always easy to tell which is the hero and which the monster. Sometimes monsters wear the forms of friends. Sometimes heroes come to save one's life and soul in the form of refugees —the kind of heroes who carry no weapon, only a kind heart. And Lengo failed to notice that he stopped taking his pills, and instead self-medicated with alcohol. Both the grandmother and the teacher failed her boy.

Her shoulders slump, but the knot in her gut reminds her she cannot linger. Now she knows where Jason has gone. Nikolas must have told him about the secret tunnels beneath the old chapel. How did *he* find out? Nikolas was only there as a toddler, after they laid his parents to rest. She thought he'd forgotten. But what matters now is that Jason has at least an hour's head start towards the chapel atop the cliffside—the chapel Lengo tends like all the women in her family did before her, since before the Romans and the Ottomans. The chapel with the blue windows and the white walls over the wine-dark sea, and the little fence that encloses a few family graves. Her grandson's too, beside the rest of their family.

She puts on her boots, her headscarf, and a heavy coat, grabs her walking stick and the flashlight she keeps by the front door, and steps out into the night.

It's a short hike uphill. A path Lengo has climbed too many times in her life, sometimes for Sunday mass when a priest still bothered to come this way. For funerals too, and for her Nikolas' baptism. More often, though, to tend to the damages the old building suffers, to whitewash its walls and keep the shutters and door from falling off their hinges. Her feet can find their way even in the dark—they did so in bloody sneakers the night Nikolas died. But tonight the raging wind howls alongside her raging heart and makes every step an ordeal. While she struggles to keep her headscarf in place and her hair from lashing her face, her eyes catch glimpses of the Unseen. Ghostly forms appear hiking beside her: her yaya has returned alongside *her* yaya's ghost, and other old-timers Lengo has no names for. The chapel has changed forms and guardians many a time: at one time it was devoted to Poseidon with white marble columns, then to Helios, since it faces East, and then to Prophet Elijah. During the Ottoman occupation, about three centuries ago, some reformed pirate captain of the Barbary Coast dedicated it to Aghios Nikolas, the patron saint of sailors.

Poseidon, Helios, Elijah, Nikolas—all of them trespassers on sacred land that belongs to an Other—someone who's never left, and remains sleeping in the depths.

The chapel's door looms open, its hinges squeaking at every gust of the wind. Lengo slips inside and bolts the door behind her. At the back of her thoughts, she's hoped she'd find Jason in here, paying his respects to his friend's memory. But no—he didn't even light a candle. The chapel is empty, filled with the scent of long-burned beeswax candles planted on brass trays of sea sand, and whiffs of frankincense. The vigil oil lamp over the sad Virgin's painting casts dancing lights at the corners of the chamber, creating angles within angles and turns within turns that shouldn't exist. Lengo adds oil to the lamp, and checks behind the never-used episcopal seat—as if any of their lazy lot would grace the place with their presence. The trapdoor behind it is open.

So Jason did discover the chapel's secret—or thinks he did.

She shouldn't waste a single minute, but she still lights a thin candle and plants it in the sand. *For Nikolas.* At the edge of her vision, she thinks she sees him as a toddler, sitting in the chapel's corner. He's playing with a wooden ship— a flimsy little thing, one of the crafts merchants sell to the tourists in summertime. He goes on and on, weaving tales of how he's going to have his own ship one day, and he'll set sail to slay the

Mermaid who drowned his parents. And then, he's over there, by the Virgin's painting, with Astur at his side on their wedding day. When she looked at him, she saw what Lengo saw: a kind heart and a traveling mind that always crafted stories within stories, so he could endure a world that had become too ugly, too soon.

Lengo wipes her tears, then sheds her coat, pockets her flashlight, and starts the descent to the tunnels beneath, her walking stick in hand. She doesn't need light where she's going; she's trodden these depths often. Her mind finds solace in the absence of light. She doesn't want to see the surface of the rock around her. She pretends that her fingers do not trace the indentations and the folds on marble and granite. A few sections here and there bear marks of human tools, and others run smooth, as if carved by monstrous, rock-drilling earthworms. She's heard from her predecessors that similar tunnels run the length of the Aegean and then some, a labyrinth that harbors hidden chambers and creatures worse than a minotaur.

One such monster has chosen to desecrate one of the labyrinth's holiest places. Deep beneath the island and the bottom of the Aegean, the tunnel opens into a narrow cavern, no bigger than the chapel above. Lengo hears curses, and through the cavern's entrance the wavering beam of a flashlight creates more uncanny angles. She stops a few paces away to remove her boots and socks. The rock beneath her feet is cold, damp, and a little slippery, and she takes tentative steps forward. The chill sends pinpricks up her legs and into her hips, but also soft vibrations of welcome.

The cavern resembles the Christian chapels that shepherds sometimes carve into the mountain caves of mainland Greece. It has a row of *stacidia* at each side—those narrow, uncomfortable seats for the congregation, a few unlit oil lamps hanging from the roof, and a single icon painted on the far wall: the Virgin holding the infant. Only this Virgin isn't depicted as the sad mother. This one is Fury-eyed, clad in black, her face stern and her head wrapped in a dark kerchief. No locks of hair hide beneath it, but a wild mane of writhing serpents. In her left hand she holds the Infant, in her right she wields the Trident. And from her waist down, she's immersed in a bottomless sea, her great tail controlling the storm.

Lengo bows her head to the Lady of the Deep. She bears many names: Panaghia Gorgona, the Madonna Mermaid. Older ones, too: Tethys, Tiamat, Thalatta. Sometimes Gorgo, sometimes Medusa, hidden in the narratives of great—*Hah!*—heroes slaying monsters. And this particular 'hero' has tossed the place apart as if seeking more hidden passageways, leading to the Lady herself.

"Kera-Lengo? What are you doing here?" Jason's bark kicks her back to reality. He frowns, and measures her from bare feet to headscarf. His voice hardens. "You knew. *You.* His yaya."

She takes another step inside, her back no longer hunched, her shoulders straight, her walking stick of sturdy cedar wood her staff and her scepter in one.

"What exactly do you think I knew, boy?"

His mouth twists, his right hand reaches behind his back—for a gun? With his left, he waves towards the painting.

"That! Nikolas told me everything! He told me how you brought him here as a child to scare him into mindless obedience. How you fed him chemicals to cloud his mind! But he always made excuses for you, painting you as another innocent victim of this monstrous cult plaguing his island. But you aren't innocent, are you? What kind of tricks did you use to lure him into the arms of that *filth*? To dilute his pure Greek bloodline into half-breed offspring?" He draws his gun and wings it about, pointing it at everything and nothing. "I told him to take care of the negr—"

"Watch it, *boy*. Don't you dare speak ill of my granddaughter-in-law."

Lengo strikes her stick on the ground. The cavern responds with a low tremor beneath their feet. In one of the side chambers, stored clay discs and tablets explain the number and sequence of blows required for an assortment of outcomes: from soft vibrations to heal, to focused earthquakes that can raise rogue waves against pirate ships at their shores. Lengo's yaya once told her of a disc with instructions to raise the Lady herself. But that was stolen long ago, and now features in the case of some museum. Lengo hasn't read even half of the tablets —some alphabets have lost their meaning by now, other tablets crumbled before anyone could copy them. And even if she tried, she'd never remember them all.

Jason scowls. "Your *arapina* grandaughter-in-law is dead. Why would you care for *that* more than your own grandson?"

"You know that they never found her body, right?"

"Nikos tossed her off the cliff into the sea, didn't he? I read the investigators' report." He sneers. "It helps to know people in the Force. She's probably fish food by now. Think of that, next time you cook fish. You might eat pieces of her. Or of her spawn." He laughs, as if he's heard the world's best joke.

Lengo sees red. She knocks the ground three times, more forcefully than she should have. An earthquake builds up in the depths, and pieces of rock crumble to the ground behind Jason. Dust sprinkles their heads, and Lengo forces her grip to remain steady.

"You idiot. You shit-souled idiot. You think we don't know how your kind often packs together within the police and armed forces? They didn't find the body because—"

"Because I'm not dead," Astur finishes Lengo's sentence.

A steady voice just behind Lengo's shoulder. Jason pales. Lengo tilts her head as much as her aching neck allows, bone grinding on bone, to meet Astur's gaze. There she is, her brave girl, clad in Lengo's old clothes that hang on her two sizes too large, but thick enough to shield her from the dampness of these tunnels. Astur carries her infant daughter on her chest, in a sling made from a colorful silk scarf that survived Nikolas' rage on that fateful night. The child naps peacefully, thank the Virgin, despite the tremors and the racket.

Lengo glances at Jason, whose eyes are fixed on Astur's head, and the black kerchief she's wrapped her hair in. Dark coils escape from the sides, much like Medusa's serpents.

"But... There was blood up the trail—"

"Because *I* put those bloody footprints on the trail to the cliff." Lengo's gut tightens as the memory of her own *Via Dolorosa* resurfaces—her hike uphill towards the cliffside across from the chapel, her feet sloshing at every step in her grandson's bloodied sneakers, her right hand dipped in Astur's blood brushing against wind-blown acacias and prickly shrubs, and her own shoes in her left for the journey back home. "But first we carried her here, where she could heal and give birth on safe, hallowed ground."

Astur takes two more steps forward, and her hand seeks Lengo's hand—the hand with the still-numb fingers after she removed the sneakers with Astur's blood on them from her grandson's dangling corpse. And now her eyes mist, her soul overflowing with secrets, grief, and guilt. It wasn't easy to carry Astur up here. May the Virgin keep them all safe, others from nearby settlements came to their aid when she called them in the middle of the night. The retired midwife, with decades of experience before hospital births caught up with the Greek countryside. Katina, Lengo's third cousin, who was a military nurse at the Albanian front during WWII. And a few others, all of them old women set on protecting their own from modern-day monsters.

Jason's eyes narrow. "Nikos killed himself for nothing. His death is on your head, monster. You did this." *Now* he looks at Astur. "You both did."

"Leave my granddaughter-in-law out of this. Yes, *I* did this."

Lengo holds her head high and her voice steady, while her heart plummets towards the depths beneath their feet, once those words leave her tongue. She should have known. She should have noticed Nikolas spiralling into delusion, self-medicating. Then she wouldn't have come home to find him black-out drunk, having burned everything Astur owned so she wouldn't leave him. She wouldn't have found Astur on the floor across the room, beaten, bruised, and weeping in a pool of blood and amniotic fluid.

Jason points the gun at Lengo. "This stops here. I'll restore Nikos' name, who died a hero, slain by monster-worshiping degenerates."

"You have no idea how Nikolas died," Lengo says. "Or how he lived." Lengo raises her chin and meets his gaze, her heart sinking deeper into a storm. Her boy died alone. Scared. In the dark, thinking himself forsaken. But... would any of this have ever happened without the poison this bastard dripped into her boy's ears? "So shut your mouth and get out while you still can."

Jason sneers. "I'm not Nikos. You cannot order me around."

A breeze against her face. The breath of the goddess? At the far corner of the room, she sees Jason in a corner, his face wet, huddling with his dog. He can't be more than twelve, but he looks older. And bigger. Lengo has seen his kind during her teaching years: the kid that's bigger than the others, always goaded to throw the first punch in a fight, always valued only as a battering ram, always mocked if he shows interest in anything remotely intellectual. A scared little orphan, yearning for a family to belong to. But maybe his own yaya died too soon, and his only friend left him. Maybe he had no one to help him find the light.

In any case, that boy is long gone. Lengo cannot help him. The man that he's become now starts to raise his gun, Astur takes a step forward and stands abreast of Lengo. Lengo moves her stick to her left hand so now both of them hold it. They hit the ground twice, the angle just so to the left, just before he pulls the trigger. The quake startles him, and he misses. The bullet hits the cavern wall an arm's length from Lengo's head, then ricochets and hits the Lady's icon on her left eye. It chips off the paint, then whooshes past Lengo's head, scraping her right ear, and flies into the tunnels behind them.

He takes aim again, but then a howl rises from the depths. It starts like a murmur within the stone—a soft, healing vibration that waxes to a whine that becomes the wail of an angered deity, rudely awaken from her slumber. What frequency did the idiot's bullet trigger, to release the wail of the goddess? Is it just her howl, or has she risen, at long last?

Jason falls on his knees, clasping the sides of his head, as if anything could stop the wail from drilling holes into his mind. It hurts Lengo too, but much less so, her own ears stiffened by age and the continued exposure to the Aegean winter's winds. Astur grunts and lets go of the stick to shield her child's ears. The memory of blood dripping from Astur's ears from Nikolas' beating crushes Lengo's heart, and fuels her wrath. But Astur shakes her head, and mouths that she's fine. Then Lengo's eyes turn to the writhing body on the floor. She and Astur cannot let this pain—or any pain—rob them of their chance.

Lengo marches to Jason, hefting her stick as a woodsman's ax, and manages a blow at the side of his head.

"When you see your Nazi friends in hell, tell them that *Outis* killed you!"

He falls sideways to the ground, his eyes unfocused, frothing at the mouth.

Astur follows her and manages a well-balanced kick to his jaw. Something cracks. Lengo brings the stick down again and again, on his head, on his back, on his chest, smashing his beefy fingers that move as if to shield him from her wrath. Every hit is a howl in her head and an apology she cannot yet bring herself to utter.

Forgive me, my Nikolas, for all my shortcomings! Forgive me, my girl, for not hiding the tickets I got you to flee from what your husband had become! Forgive me for not being there, when he found them, to take the beating instead of you!

Lengo beats Jason until she's run out of breath, until she's run out of tears, until he's running out of life—until a steady hand grips the stick mid-blow. Lengo turns to Astur, a yell building up in her throat. How dare she deny Lengo her revenge?

In the strange shadows cast by the discarded flashlight, the tendrils beneath Astur's scarf seem to slither and writhe around her head and neck, like the Lady's serpents on the wall behind them. The moisture in Lengo's eyes blurs the two forms, as though Astur now stands in the Lady's embrace, slithering serpents coiling around the girl's narrow shoulders, careful and affectionate as a mother's arms around her newborn.

"Please, Yaya. Let's... let's just go home. It's been forty days already." A shadow passes behind Astur's eyes, and she clutches her fussing infant tighter to her chest, without releasing Lengo's stick. "Enough with the blood. Enough with the pain. Enough with the death. Just... enough."

Lengo allows her shoulders to relax. Forty days, already... Forty days for a woman who's given birth to remain isolated from the perils of the outside world. Forty nights between death and the saranta memorial service, to ensure a spirit's safe passage to the Afterlife. And forty waves to cleanse spilled blood from one's hands. But where to find compassion in the storm that rages in her heart? She raises her gaze to Astur and, at the edge of her vision, something sparkles: the Lady's left eye. A reflection of the lamplight on some quartz crystal embedded in the rock? Or has her face mellowed? The great tail of the Virgin All-mother commands the storm, but also calms the waves.

"How can you say this, love? He doesn't deserve mercy."

Astur sighs. "For his own yaya, then. For her memory."

"At least she didn't fail him. Like I did."

Astur lets go of the stick. "Don't ever say that, yaya." She holds her baby with both hands and brings it closer to Lengo's face. "*She* is not a failure. She's here because of you. You cannot save those who don't want to be saved."

But what if Jason does? And she failed to see it? Lengo's eyes well up. The stick slips from her grip and she drops to her knees, the weight of the world crushing her shoulders. Between sobs, she blurts out the silliest thing.

"He… he ate the rice I made for you! I-I have nothing for you when you come home!"

A soft embrace around Lengo's shaking shoulders, tendrils of hair and slithering serpents and a cooing child near her arm.

"Then we'll make more. Come, Yaya. Let's go home."

"And what about him?"

"He's in the Lady's arms now. She'll heal his body, as she's healed mine. But his heart and mind… that's on him."

He doesn't deserve it—nothing has convinced Lengo that he does. But she sighs, and nods, and gets up to roll his body onto thick sailcloth. Then they drag him out of the chapel on the slippery tunnel floor further down, to one of the healing chambers below. If the Lady deems him worthy one day, she may lead him out to the light again. Unless...

Unless Lengo becomes a teacher again. Unless she too takes the long road towards redemption, and she makes the time to guide this foolish boy back to the light. Or, at least, try to. She has many long days and even longer nights ahead of her, but the first step towards healing has always been mercy. Lengo sets him on a cot of riggings, sailcloth, and fishnets, she leans and whispers in his ear the first of his many lessons on monsters and heroes.

"Whenever you see your Nazi pals again, in this life or the next, tell them that Medusa showed you mercy, where you showed her none."

But she makes sure she takes her walking stick with her, when they start their way home. And she'll make another one, for Astur. A good, sturdy staff.

Just in case.

See Christine Lucas's story "Medusa Rising" online at Metaphorosis.
If you liked it, leave a comment. Authors love that!
Remember to subscribe to our e-mail updates so you'll know when new stories are posted.

About the story

"Medusa Rising" is inspired by H.P.Lovecraft's story "Medusa's Coil", mostly known for its racist ending. The premise was stuck in my head when, back in 2019, the legal proceedings against the Greek Neo-Nazi Party Golden Dawn began. Then it became clear in my head who the evil guys were, and who Medusa had to represent. Greek Grandmothers have stood against fascists for a long time (and still do). The first draft of the story flowed onto the screen within a single day, because it's a theme very dear to my heart.

A question for the author

Q: What are you reading now?

A: *A Night in the Lonesome October* by R. Zelazny. It's one of my comfort reads when I'm feeling down, because Snuff's (the canine protagonist) voice is so honest and clear that brings everything together. Of course it also includes cats, the Dreamlands, and a cast of familiar and yet unexpected characters. It's an easy, entertaining read that gives me hope that everything will be well at the end.

About the author

Christine Lucas lives in Greece with her life partner and a horde of spoiled animals. She's a retired Air Force officer (disabled) and mostly self-taught in English. Her work appears in several print and online magazines, including *Future SF Digest, Pseudopod,* and *Strange Horizons*. She was a finalist for the 2017 WSFA award, and a collection of her short stories, titled *Fates and Furies,* was published in late 2019 by Candlemark & Gleam.

werecat99.wordpress.com, @ChrisLuc99

From a Mother to Her Daughter, on the Eve of Her Wedding

Elliott Gish

May 8, 1888

My dearest Louisa,

By the time you read this letter, the most wonderful day of your life will be over, and night will have stolen over the grand, grey house that you must now call your own. In my mind I clearly perceive you sitting by a yawning fireplace, shivering a little in the chill of the spring evening. Above you, gloom; behind you, dimly looming, the wide stretch of your marriage-bed.

What will you be doing? Here my imagination fails me; it has never been powerful. I recall clearly the times when you begged me to tell you stories as a girl, only to roll your eyes and harrumph when I offered you the well-worn tales I knew from nursery books. "Not a story like that!" you would cry, your face puckered and displeased. "A new one!" And you would fuss, and kick, and pinch, until finally I sent you off to bed in hopes that you would sleep away your fit of temper. I never had a new story to offer you, my darling, and for that I am sorry.

Your husband being elsewhere, attending to some man's affair, I hope that you will finally grow weary of waiting for him, just as you used to grow weary of waiting for me when I could not keep up with you during a walk or a game. Up you will get to walk off a bout of nerves, pacing to and fro, until your eyes come to rest on your hope chest, cold and forlorn in the corner of the room. (How I pray that it is there, and not abandoned in some hallway, or left to gather dust beneath the stairs!) Your gaze will slide along its elegant cedar panels, the rich curves of your initials carved into the wood, and you will be moved to cross the bedchamber and throw open its lid. There you will find this letter, tightly sealed with wax, nestled comfortably atop your muslin nightgown.

Louisa—stop now and listen. Are there footsteps in the passage? Can you feel eyes staring at you through a crack in the door? Are you certain that you are alone? If so, read on, for at last I have a new story.

When, as a girl, you first became interested in this alien thing called Love, you asked about how your father and I met, how we courted, why we married. My reply was so meagrely furnished with detail that you wandered away before I finished, throwing over your shoulder a scornful remark about my lack of romantic feeling. But although you have only ever known me as a staid old matron, I was once a girl like you, brimming with fire and honey, so full of passion that I scarcely knew what to do with myself. It was in this state that I met your father, on a warm summer evening at a garden party.

Even from a distance, he was the most beautiful thing I had ever seen. Slim and tall, with dark gold hair and dark brown eyes, a firm chin and a soft, girlish mouth. I watched him cross the lawn with a swift, sure stride, stopping here and there to briefly greet a gentleman of his acquaintance, or drop a careless compliment in the lap of a pretty girl. He seemed to be a man with a destination. What that destination might be, I could only imagine; and, as I have said already, imagination is not my strong suit. I know it is yours, so perhaps you can imagine my surprise when this angelic creature stopped directly in front of me. His nostrils flared slightly, as though he inhaled my scent, and he smiled.

"We do not know each other, I think," he said. I remember those words as clearly now as I did that night in bed, hearing them echo sweetly in my ears. His left hand bore a silver signet ring on its smallest finger, set with three brilliant yellow jewels, two large, one small. It winked in the sun every time he shifted his grip on his walking-stick, flashing like a Morse lamp, a beckoning call in a code I could not read.

I shall spare you further details of our courtship, our outings and walks and conversations; no mother may hold her daughter's attention with such tedious remembrances. Suffice to say that by the time he proposed—as he did, after seeking your grandfather's permission for my hand—I had been thoroughly wooed, and accepted with scarcely a flutter of nerves. My days became lightsome and busy, filled with those duties so particular to brides—the same duties that have filled your life these past few weeks, my darling, as you strained your eyes and pricked your fingers embroidering handkerchiefs and hemming linen and sewing flounces of lace to your bridal-gown.

"I cannot sew a moment longer!" you shouted only days ago, so carried away by temper that I thought you might tear the dress up and kick it into the hearth. But soon enough your anger ebbed, and you became again distracted by dreams of your husband-to-be.

On the morning of my wedding, rather than walking a short distance to my old village church, I climbed into your father's carriage for a long journey across the moors; it was, I had been told, a custom of his family that brides would be married in the family chapel. How I shivered when I first saw the vast black hump of my new home, huddled on the horizon like a sleeping giant! It was so large that I could see it for a good hour, and felt almost as though *it* approached *me*, not the other way around. The closer it drew, the more my nerves began, finally, to flutter, and the more I began to wish that I were back at home, tucked safely into my virgin bed.

But such thoughts are common to brides, and when I began my walk down the aisle and saw your father waiting for me at the end of it, all ivory and gold, my girlish fears evaporated. I did not mind the draftiness of the chapel, or the incoherent mumbling of its ancient vicar. I did not mind the strange wine we were bidden to drink at the altar, which tasted both bitter and sweet. I did not mind the way my husband's guests—all of them men, and family, I assumed, for they shared his golden beauty, and wore the same silver ring with three yellow stones upon their fingers—watched my every move, scarcely blinking. All that mattered was that I was his now, to have and to hold, to honour and to cherish—that I was now, at last, a Wife! So eager was I to have your father to myself that I rather chafed at the celebration that followed the wedding. I could not stop my teeth from gritting, nor my eyes from narrowing at anyone who chose to have another glass of champagne, another slice of cake,

another turn around the ballroom. Why
could these people not disperse, I
wondered, and let me enjoy my wedding-
night?

At last the guests began to yawn, and
one by one they made their excuses, bade
us good fortune, and stumbled out into
the night. I had been longing for them to
leave all evening, and yet, now that my
wish was granted and I was finally alone
with my husband, I was suddenly shy.

Your father, however, seemed to know
what to do. He kissed me briefly—only our
second kiss, for he had waited until we
met at the altar to kiss me for the first
time—and told me to take the greater
staircase up to the second floor. "Your
bedroom," he said, "is the third door from
the left. Obey the instructions on the
bedside table, and in time, I will come to
you."

I puzzled over these words as I climbed
towards my destination. Why was it to be
my bedroom, and not *ours*? Were we not
to sleep in one bed, as behooved a couple
united in wedlock?

The bedroom that was to be mine was
very grand and very gloomy, with only a
single candle burning on the bedside table

to give its shadows depth. A crisply folded piece of your father's stationery was propped up beside it. I opened it and saw, in your father's neat hand, the following instructions:

Remove your clothing.
Extinguish the candle.
Draw the bag over your head.
Wait on the bed.

The bag in question I found on the eiderdown. It was a little sack, such as one that might hold flour, with a drawstring in its mouth so that it could be pulled tight around the neck.

Faced with such a queer catalogue of demands, perhaps you, Louisa, would not acquiesce; perhaps you, more brazen than I, would storm downstairs and confront your husband, demanding to know what he meant by such a list. But I was not like you, and so I did not think to disobey. I removed my wedding-dress—a difficult feat, as no maid attended me, and it fastened with two dozen tiny pearl buttons —and my petticoats, and finally, reluctantly, my unmentionables. Unclad, I felt at once the draft in that great room, and I shivered as I blew out the candle, pulled the bag over my head, and felt my

way to the foreign bed, mounting it
clumsily in the darkness.

After my engagement, my mother had
made occasional opaque references to 'the
state of wifehood', vaguely insinuating
that my transition into this state would
take place, not at the altar, or during the
signing of the registry, but over the course
of the wedding-night. I must confess that I
had some faint inkling of what this state
might entail; during my childhood I had
often seen animals enacting their strange
rituals of courtship in yard and field. My
childish brain recognized the connection
between these curious animal dances and
the later arrival of kittens, piglets, foals,
and calves. I was able to eventually draw
a parallel between this state of affairs and
that of Marriage—to understand, in a dim,
unfocused way, that since a Woman
united with a Man in wedlock will usually
bear children, a similar dance must take
place between them. This I pondered as I
lay in the dark, the bag firmly drawn over
my head, trying to imagine what change
awaited me when your father entered the
room.

I have no way of knowing how long,
dear Louisa, I lay upon that bed before

your father came into the room. The long wait had made me fretful and nervous, and when the chamber door flew open with a bang, I could not help but shriek in fear, my body on that enormous bed jerking as though shot through with lightning.

"You must lie very still," he said, and his voice was suddenly much colder than it had been hours before, when we had exchanged our wedding-vows. And thus our night began.

My daughter, to frighten you is not my aim, nor yet my purpose in this letter, and yet I must tell you that until that night, I did not know what Pain was. The unitary act, of which I was so ignorant, provoked in me such a feeling of terror and agony that I felt I would be ripped down the middle like a paper doll. With the bag over my head and no candles lit beyond I could see nothing, not even the dimmest outline of your father's face, but I could hear his harsh and ragged breath, the stream of unintelligible words he muttered as he laid his weight upon me; and it seemed to me that he had not two hands but dozens, all emerging from the darkness to pin my shaking limbs to the bed, gripping them so tightly I was sure the nails would

pierce the skin—and so they had, I saw
the next day, when I examined myself
before the mirror and beheld a number of
deep punctures in my arms and legs, the
skin around them purple and bruised.

I writhed—I wept—I begged your father
for mercy, and received none. He said not
a word to me throughout this torturous
ordeal, neither of comfort for my weeping
nor of remonstrance for my inability to
remain still. It seemed to me that many
painful hours went by while he thrust and
poked and grappled with my flesh as
though he were the Devil himself, until
finally he let out a long, strange moan, his
hands gripping ever tighter until the
sound abruptly ceased. In the darkness
beneath my hood, I heard him sigh, then
felt the burning weight of him leave me.

Footsteps creaked away across the
bedroom floor. The door opened, then
shut. He did not say goodnight, nor bid
me well. He did not even remove the bag.

I hope to never again have a night as
wretched as that one. Alone, unclothed, I
abandoned myself to a wild fit of hysterics
that went unnoticed in that great house. I
am sure that my weeping could be heard
in every room, but no one came to comfort

me—not your father, not a servant, not even a curious dog. Loneliness weighed so heavy on my soul that I felt as though *he* lay upon me still.

Oh, how I shuddered when I saw your father there at the breakfast-table the next morning! He was as handsome, as golden, as charming as ever, but the sight of him made me shiver all over, like a dog who, having once been kicked, trembles to see its master.

We broke our fast in silence, attended by his grim, grey servants. Questions roiled within my unsettled mind, so pressing and urgent that I felt I might burst with them. How could he who had only yesterday promised to love and care for me have hurt me so dreadfully, ignored my cries of protest with such a will? How could he sit there calmly with his coffee and his paper after my person had been so grotesquely outraged? How, how, how could he act as though all was well, when nothing was well, and never would be again?

The next few months of my life felt like a hideous dream. During the day, I would wander the manor, some servant always trailing silently behind me. During the evening I ate dinner with your father, who often brought his friends with their silver rings to eat with us; they spoke together in a language I did not know, all hissing consonants and harsh, spitting vowels. At nightfall I would enter my bedroom with a thumping heart, my eyes landing immediately on that hideous table to see if it bore another folded note, bidding me to strip, blind myself, and wait. There was no logic to these nights as far as I could tell, no pattern I could learn that might allow me to steel myself. Sometimes he would appear five nights in a row, leaving me so sore I could barely stir from my bed; then he would abstain for weeks, even months, until I began to think that perhaps I was free of his hideous attentions forever.

And then, inevitably, a note would appear on the bedside table, and a bag on the bed, and the horror would begin once more.

I tried to explore my new abode, but many of the doors were locked, and sometimes even if they were not, whatever servant accompanied me would step before me and prevent me from entering, telling me that my husband had declared it 'out of bounds'. The library was out of bounds. My husband's room and study were out of bounds. Conservatory, parlour, drawing room, dining room, nursery, even the kitchen and the scullery were off-limits to me when not in the company of my husband.

"I am the mistress of this house!" I cried one day, frustrated by the constant barrage of refusal; and the servant who had denied me entrance said, without missing a beat:

"Yes, madam, but you see, he is its *master*, and yours, too."

One of the few places I was permitted was the long gallery. On days that were cold or rainy I would walk there to get my exercise, gazing up at the portraits that lined walls at regular intervals, your father's ancestors stately and beautiful as angels. All of them, I saw, bore silver rings on their left hands, the stones as golden as their hair. The terrace was also within my accepted bounds, as were the gardens scattered across the house's sprawling grounds. Ordinary, orderly gardens they were, full of roses and hollyhocks, wisteria and foxglove—and yet there were stranger blossoms scattered throughout, monstrously large and tinged with foreign colours whose names I did not know, their perfume so delicate and strange it made me swoon.

On one occasion I plucked one of these flowers and set it in a vase beside my bed, wanting to fill the air with that curious scent. I dreamed that night of another garden, somewhere far away. In the distance I could see the shadowy outlines of ruined towers, as though I stood in the pleasure-garden of a palace only recently brought tumbling down by Time. Those mysterious flowers bloomed all around me, making the air hazy with scent. When I looked upwards, instead of a single sun, I saw *three*: two large, one small, burning in a sky whose colour was all wrong.

I woke up the next morning with a ferocious headache, and the vase on the table quite empty. A servant stood at the foot of my bed, looking dourly upon me.

"The master says the flowers ain't to be plucked," she said.

I never picked a flower on the grounds of your father's house again, although that dream came back to me over and over.

My dear, are you *quite* sure that there is no one else present? Have you checked beneath the bed? in the wardrobe? behind the chiffonier? Are those drapes stirring faintly in a draft coming from the window, or do they conceal some gleeful spy?

Never mind. I must trust you to know that your solitude is complete.

When I had been married for nearly a year, I found another folded note on my bedside table. I removed my clothes, eased the bag over my head, and blew out the candle before climbing onto the bed. However, I found as I lay back on the bed that I had not pulled the drawstring as tight as usual, and that if I lay with my head far back on the pillow and my chin tight against my neck, I was able to peep through the slit at the bottom of the bag. It was a full moon, the room so brightly lit it was almost like day, but I could see little enough: my own body pimpling in the chill of the room, a sliver of bedpost and curtain, a hint of the darkness beyond.

I was reaching up to pull the drawstring tight around my throat when I heard the creaking of feet coming down the passage. Hastily I returned my hand to its resting place on the eiderdown, just in time for your father to make his entrance.

I saw only the briefest of glimpses from my accidental peephole. A cloth of some kind thrown carelessly onto the floor; a patch of skin, silver-white in the moonlight; and then he began his usual line of attacks on my person. By now I was so used to these nighttime ministrations that they had become almost dull. Even though I still felt my body seize in terror at his approach, even though the smell of him still filled me with loathing, I found myself bored by his efforts, and by my feelings of panic and dismay. The reactions of my body wearied me; I was left cold by my own suffering.

And then one of your father's hands slipped, catching on the loose sackcloth gathered at the top of my head, and the bag pulled inadvertently up over my chin, my nose, my eyes. And I could see all.

The thing that straddled my body in the moonlight was no man. Its eyes were your father's, and its smell, and its voice mumbling words in no language I had ever learned; but the face was long and thin, the mouth a lipless gash, the nose no more than twin holes in its face. The body was painfully slender, grey-white skin pulled tight over tendon and bone, with arms (and it seemed to me that there were more than two, Louisa!) ending in grasping talons, grabbing greedy handfuls of my flesh and twisting it as though they meant to tear it off in lumps. Between the cadaverous legs, sliding in and out of me, was its member, a thing that I cannot describe—not out of feminine decorum, but because the sight of it so horrified me that I could not keep the image of it in my head. Even now I am unable to picture it, try as I might. All I can see is a mess of wormy skin, exposed nerve, pulsing muscle.

This glimpse of your father's true form lasted only a moment, and then his eyes met mine, and whatever impulse had frozen me in place disappeared. I screamed, long and louder than I had ever screamed before, and he screamed too, the thin slash of his mouth gaping impossibly wide into a great black hole. He scuttled away from me like some monstrous crab, back and back until he fell off the bed and onto the stone floor. After a moment he stood, pulling a length of cloth around him like a robe—and then I saw it was not cloth at all, but *skin*, the same skin he had discarded moments ago. He was wrapping himself in human flesh, swaddling his grotesque body in the shape that I had come to know as my lawful husband. In a moment he stood before me as I had always seen him, beautiful and fair, his silver ring winking in the moonlight. He looked at me, his face twisted as though he was as horrified as I was, then turned tail and fled the room, oaths in that unknown language dripping from his tongue.

I did not want to go downstairs the next morning; I had no wish to share a room with that *thing*, knowing now what lay under the beautiful skin. But go I did, forced downstairs and into my seat by your father's servants and their strong, cruel hands. Your father watched them manhandle me into my chair, drinking a cup of coffee. The agitation of the night before seemed to have left him; he looked entirely calm.

"You were not meant to see what you saw last night," he said.

This was so obvious a statement—the snuffed candle! the bag!—that I could not suppress a bark of laughter. He registered this with barely a twitch of his elegant eyebrows.

"The proper thing to do," he continued, "would be to kill you. That is the usual consequence of women spying on that which does not concern them."

The silence that followed these words seemed to have a tangible weight, pressing on my eardrums as though I were suddenly underwater. Your father took a sip of coffee and hummed under his breath.

"However," he said, "there is the matter of the child to consider."

My face in that moment, I am sure, was as blank as any woman's face could be. "The what?" I said.

"You are pregnant," he said, and smiled, the same smile that had so captivated me upon our first meeting. Just as they had then, his nostrils flared. "Even after one night, I can smell my seed finally taking root in you."

I winced at his crudeness—and winced again as I thought of how I had come to be in such a state, how brutally he had used me.

"And so," he continued, "you have two choices. You may leave, remove yourself to your father's house, if he will have you, or wander the streets as a beggar or a whore, if he will not. You may birth my child in filth and squalor, knowing that when you do, I will snatch him from your arms and drown you in the nearest river. And make no mistake, I will do this. Should you go to France, or Bohemia, or Timbuktu, *I will find you*, and I will take what is mine. According to the laws of my people—and yours, I believe—a child is the rightful property of his father. The mother is merely the vessel through which he enters the world, the jug from which the water pours."

My people, he said. But what people were those? I remembered, suddenly, the dreams that had plagued me after plucking that strange flower, the vision of that faraway garden under three burning suns, that palace crumbling into dust. The three stones on your father's ring caught the morning light as he took a sip of coffee.

"And what," I asked, "is the second choice?"

"To be the lady of this house," he replied. "To lie with me without complaint, to bear the children that will bear my name, to appear by my side when I need you to and disappear when I do not. Do these things, and you will live in comfort for the rest of your life—although it will be short, as all your kind's lives are."

"Shall I live in safety, as well as comfort?" I asked, and now it was his turn to laugh.

"These are your choices, wife," he said. "Live with me knowing that I could kill you, or run from me knowing that I will."

I have never been brave. I made my choice.

For thirteen months I carried you, longer than any woman is meant to carry a human child. Your father's strange friends would appear at all hours of the day and night, pressing their elegant hands to my stomach, saying not a word to me but toasting your father with glasses of bittersweet wine, praising his virility in that language I did not know. "A son!" they cried, their rings glittering in the lamplight, "a son!" And I pictured a ghoulish creature like your father sliding out of my womb, and wept.

But of course, you were no son, and when, after a day and a night of labour, I finally looked into your little pink face, I felt myself overcome with relief and fear in equal measure. Relief, because you were a human girl-child, and not some unholy wraith; and fear, because I had no inkling of how your father would react to a daughter. When he saw you, however, he only shrugged and said, "A girl may have her uses, given time."

He continued to visit me at night, trying to beget a son, but your time inside my body seemed to have robbed it of its creative powers. Still, I called for hot water whenever he left me to rid myself of his stink and seed, and made the servants brew me thick cups of pennyroyal tea, to make sure that no other child could take root.

Louisa, you were the only thing in that hideous house for me to love, and I loved you with all the strength I had. I insisted on feeding you from my own breast. Although your father soon procured a stone-faced woman to act as your nursemaid, I kept you by my side whenever I could, letting her trail wordlessly behind us as we frolicked. I taught you how to read with the wizened letter-blocks from my own childhood nursery. We played hide-and-seek in the gardens, tag in the echoing ballroom, ran footraces along the marble length of the long gallery, your father's ancestors smiling down at us from within their ornate frames. As a toddling thing you paid them no mind, but as you grew older you began to look at them more closely, squinting up through the gloom at those fair and winsome faces. Once, I recall, you turned to me and asked:

"Mamma, why are there no ladies in any of these pictures?"

It startled me, that question, for until that moment I had not noticed that, indeed, the portraits were all of gentlemen. Not a single woman stared down from that gallery wall.

The older you grew, the more I understood how unlike me you were: brash instead of meek, bright instead of dull, bold instead of timid. You were not afraid to ask questions, even when I could not or would not answer them. When you split your chin on the edge of a table, you scarcely cried; when you tripped over a loose cobble and broke your wrist trying to catch yourself, you let the doctor set it without a murmur of complaint. You climbed to the top of the tallest trees, dove into the coldest lakes, approached the wildest snarling dogs with your hand outstretched, offering friendship. I have been blessed to be your mother, my brave and beautiful darling.

Louisa, I need you to be brave now, for I am approaching the heart of the matter.

Your father paid you no attention when you were a child, nor yet when you were a girl; but as you approached womanhood, he suddenly took an interest in your habits, your manners, your bearing and dress. You recall that at the supper-table —the only meal we all took together, and that rarely—he began to correct your posture, to ask you what you were reading, to observe your growing body and comment upon its form, its fullness. "You will be an easy mother," he said to you once, looking at your broad hips, and you flushed and looked ashamed.

"What did he mean?" you asked me later, sounding so puzzled and unhappy that I had to stifle the urge to run to your father and wrap my hands around his throat.

Your father's friends, too, began to lay eyes upon you in all your blooming glory. You were a sheltered baby, and you had grown into a sheltered girl; I was terrified that one of these men would request your hand, and that, knowing no other men nor any other way of life, you would oblige him. I did not know for certain if they were of a kind with your father, if they, too, had wrapped themselves in man-skins to hide their proper forms, but I had seen their rings, and I did not trust them. Therefore I determined that you must have a proper coming-out party, as is customary for a young lady of your status, and sent dozens of invitations throughout the county, hoping that one of them would be received by an eligible bachelor. Marriage had destroyed my life. I prayed it might save yours.

You remember your coming out party, I hope—your beautiful gown of pale China silk, the freesias twined through your golden hair, the scores and scores of people in the ballroom who applauded you as you made your blushing way through the door, shy for the first time in your life. Your father's friends were there in droves, but they were at last outnumbered, and my spirits lifted as I saw you speak to several eligible young men. There was one, I noticed, at whom you looked again and again, and who left your side but rarely that whole night—a handsome fellow with jet-black hair and eyes the colour of smoke. He wore the most elegant kid gloves, fastened at the wrist with cunning jet buttons, and when, later that night, I

caught him alone and let him know that
he was welcome at the Manor any time he
chose to visit, he caught my hand with his
gloved ones and kissed my fingers with
gratitude and delight.

Visit he did, often and eagerly. From
my window I watched the two of you stroll
through the gardens, resolutely followed
by your nursemaid, and felt a lightness in
my heart that I had not known for years. I
knew little of the young man, but what I
did know I liked: he was clever and
courteous, quick to joke but not to offend;
he was rich, though not terribly so, and
had political aspirations; he spoke lovingly
of his family home some miles away, the
beautiful gardens on its grounds. His
name sprang to your lips, unbidden, at
least five times a day; I admit, sometimes I
would let our conversations wander in a
way that I knew would draw your mind to
him, and then smiled to myself when you
mentioned him again. I had high hopes
that you had formed an attachment, and
when you came to me and told me that he
had proposed, I urged you to accept. I had
visions of you spirited safely away, to your
fiancé's family home or even the Capitol,
free at last—free at last!

Your engagement party was a smaller affair than your coming-out party, but still memorable for being one of the few merry occasions at your father's house. You were so lovely that evening, so clearly infatuated with your betrothed, that I could scarcely stop smiling. But I believe your fiancé smiled wider as he lifted his glass to toast your impending nuptials, your future happiness, and the blessing he had found in you, the sweetest of brides.

It was then I realized that he had not worn his gloves that evening. On the smallest finger of his left hand, gleaming in the light of the candelabra, was a silver ring set with three yellow stones.

I should have spoken to you that night, but I was frozen by my realization—frozen, and then shamed for the part I had played in it. Every day since then I have tried to speak to you alone, but it seemed that suddenly the servants attended your every waking moment, surrounding you like a cloud of houseflies. I had no chance to warn you, no opportunity to make right, until now.

I am writing this in the still hours of the morning of your wedding; the whole affair will be over when you read this letter. I can picture you in bridal-gown, its pink silk bringing out the innocent bloom of your cheeks. You will look beautiful, of course, and a little nervous, and young— this above all, for no one looks younger to a mother than her daughter. When I see you, it is not as the woman of nineteen that you are, but as many versions of yourself, one nested inside the other like those cunning Russian dolls. Yourself at fourteen, thickly flushed with blood—ten, swift and nimble as a boy—six, earnest and gap-toothed. And in the middle, in the heart, yourself as a baby, red and sticky with the mess of the womb. My own, my flesh.

Louisa, *you must not have a wedding-night*. I lost my youth to a silver ring. I will not see you lose yours, too.

When you have finished reading, put on your shoes and cloak as quietly as you can, and slip out of your bedchamber. Walk silent as a ghost down the stairs and out the door. Stay low to the ground and run towards the road, keeping to the shadows. I will be waiting there, my darling, with a horse and cart stolen from your father's stables, and together we shall take our leave of these hideous creatures.

I have no idea where we shall go. I do not know if we will be safe from our husbands on the Continent, or in India, or South Africa, or Australia. I do not know if we shall manage to escape at all. You could be caught, or I could, or we could be captured together after we meet on the road or found later in some inn or on a ship. There are infinite possibilities, and a great many of them are ugly. But I will be brave for you, my daughter—for the first time in my life, I shall be brave.

With all my love,
Your Mother

See Elliott Gish's story "From a Mother to Her Daughter, on the Eve of Her Wedding" online at Metaphorosis.
If you liked it, leave a comment. Authors love that!
Remember to subscribe to our e-mail updates so you'll know when new stories are posted.

About the story

While reading a book about Victorian social and sexual mores as research for another project, I began to think of how uninformed young women in that period were, even on their wedding nights. In such a repressed and sexually anxious society, much of the information a young woman brought with her to the bedroom would have been the result of her mother having "the talk" with her beforehand. What if that talk was not just a way for a mother to explain physical intimacy to her daughter, but to warn her about something more sinister?

A question for the author

Q: Do you make art other than prose? What kind, and how is it different?

A: My attempts at art other than prose have not been successful. My drawings are bad, my poems are worse, and the less said about my attempts at songwriting, the better. However, I did once make my mother a beaded keychain in the shape of a gecko, and it came out splendidly.

About the author

Elliott Gish is a writer and librarian from Nova Scotia. A graduate of Simon Fraser University's Writer's Studio program, her goal is to make her readers afraid to sleep without the lights on. She lives in Halifax with her partner.

www.elliottgishwrites.com, @Elliott_Gish

Midnight's Second Station

Chloe Smith

Errant had studied the reports, had marveled, had thought he'd understood as much as anyone did—but his eyes still rejected their first sight of Midnight's trees.

He squinted down through the shuttle's window. A few hours before sunset, the passing terrain was a crumpled expanse of ashy browns and pinks, covered by the pale, irregular blooms of fungal webs and the fine, regular lines of insulated pipes. Interspersed among both of these patterns, though, was another: an array of shapes cut out of absolute darkness. As much as Errant tried to make out gradations of color or get a sense of form, he saw only absence, shapes like holes gnawed through to the realm of antimatter, even as the pilot angled their craft downward and the ground rose to meet them.

They landed beside a pipeline that had looked threadlike from the air but turned out to be at least half Errant's height. It stretched away behind them, over the horizon and towards the power station's reservoir, half a hemisphere away. Just ahead, it crossed a stripe of white paint and disappeared behind the matte silhouette. Errant leaned forward, trying to see where the human creation and alien thing met, and asked the shuttle's other passenger, "What does the line signify?"

Supervisor Heren, Positive Delta Energy's ranking onsite employee and one of the only survivors of the explosion, snorted. "Safety. Rules say we need a 10-meter perimeter. Of course, they also say to monitor trunk surface temperatures."

"And you can't do both?" Cygni Authority had hired Errant as a safety inspector because he could analyze complex systems, trace the impacts and risks of human interactions with strange new biomes. In practice, a lot of that meant pinpointing profit-driven cheats and paradoxes in corporate policies.

Heren's tone was all vinegar. "We can't do the work from a distance. The perimeter rule's just a way for PD to cover their—" She cut off, and her eyes, framed within the narrow opening of her lifted viewplate, flickered towards the pilot.

Her crewmate just leaned back from her controls with a sigh. Errant didn't think he'd heard her say more than five words together in the two days he'd been down this gravity well.

Heren shook herself. "It's fine. Like I said, we have to do it regularly. Those reports I *assume* you read through don't show any correlation between the explosions and us touching the trees."

"I remember." Errant heard the defensive note in his own voice and wanted to cringe. He should be used to wiping metaphorical spit off his face. Cygni was the only interplanetary body with enough leverage to force inspections, and maybe even change, on companies like Positive Delta Energy. When he'd started visiting sites, he'd thought workers would understand he was there to help, but experience had taught him that most assumed him to be an enemy, looking for "gotcha" moments. From their perspective, his report would most likely be toothless or, at worst, an excuse for Positive Delta to fire them all.

That won't happen. That's not what I'm here for! I'm going to help keep you safe, so no one else dies. He recognized the impulse to babble assurances, ignored it.

You always care too much, Stephen said, in his head. He forced the memory down, along with the messy emotions it unleashed. This was work. He could only do his best to understand what was really happening here on Midnight. He lowered his own viewplate and turned on his comm. "I'd like to get closer, then."

But he hesitated once his boots hit soil, staring up at the void-shape before them. Its edges shifted in the wind of Midnight's thin atmosphere, ragged bits of shadow lifting and settling back.

"Don't forget to change your settings to infrared." Heren's words were still clipped, but there was none of the animus he'd heard before. It made him wonder. Maybe she *didn't* hate him on principle.

Then he switched his settings and stopped thinking about anything else.

The landscape around them faded to crepuscular greys, but the tree's utter blackness resolved a fraction. Errant squinted. He could just make out the suggestion of features—leaves moving against each other and the curve of the trunk beneath them even clearer. He took a cautious step forward, boots over the perimeter line, and another step, and another, until he could put one hand on the trunk. He felt the barest suggestion of heat, transmitted through the fierce insulation of the tree's surface and the protection of his gloves.

"It's hard to makes sense of, isn't it?" Heren's question surprised him again.

"Yes." He still felt the need to defend himself. "I did my research, you know. I don't make it a habit to charge blindly into projects involving unique xenobiology, especially when the organisms generate this much power."

There was nothing like Midnight's trees anywhere else. A plant-analog that absorbed such a complete spectrum of light shouldn't be able to exist. And yet here were the trees, with their blacker-than-black leaves and inscrutable trunks, insulating and protecting the explosively charged cores within them.

"Everyone's overawed at the start," Heren said. "The first tappers who went in to drill the siphons and lay pipe, they couldn't get over how uncanny it all was. Soren said—" She stopped again. Soren was the name of the first station's supervisor. One of the dead.

Errant pulled back, torn between two investigatory desires. On his long transport ride to Midnight, he'd studied two documents to the point of near memorization. One was the anonymous message to Cygni's Planetary Resource Operations department that had launched this inquiry. The other was Heren's post-accident debrief, a series of monosyllabic responses to the company rep's leading questions. He knew he'd have to re-interview her about what happened, to get more than the pain-filled silences between her answers. He'd been dreading it. And here she was giving him an opening—at the moment when he really needed to focus on the facts of the physical environment. He tried to approach both topics at once, and bungled it.

"There's no explanation of how they manage not to overheat, right? There weren't any clear indicators, before, when the heat control failed?"

Even faceless inside her helmet, he still *felt* the look she gave him. "No, Inspector. We don't have any certain way to predict the explosions. Don't you think, if we could have anticipated a blast—" Her gloves fisted at her sides.

Elda the pilot spoke up on the channel. "Time to inspect, Inspector."

Errant hesitated, tried to think of a way to walk back his words, and gave it up. "Right."

He returned to the tree, circled it with fingers trailing against the not-bark. The siphon jutted out at waist height on its far side, half-hidden in the artificial dimness. Once he remembered to toggle the infrared off, it seemed to float, a crisp shape even in the afternoon light, against the matte blackness. The tap line that stretched down the trunk from the spigot was just as distinct. It ran over the few meters of uneven ground between tree and pipe, a vein in the larger network.

"This tree's fallow right now." Heren had moved up beside him, and tapped the meter-transmitter on the spigot's crest. "PD rule is to give each tree a local-year off. The idea is to prevent the power gradient from becoming unsustainable."

"Do you know how they settled on these safety guidelines?" Errant asked.

"Do you?" her voice had returned to its low-grade caustic register. Errant wanted to follow up, to push her for thoughts on the soundness of company safety policies, but he was wary of another misstep. *Focus on the physical inspection, for now.*

He dropped to one knee and began digging his bots out of his pack. Humans were complicated messes of conflicting ideas, intentions, and understandings. Bots, by comparison, were much easier. And these bots were very straightforward. They just wanted to take readings and broadcast them to his terminal back at the power station. He set them in a row on the ground, where they unfolded jointed legs and began scurrying around.

"Those little guys might not make it long enough to give you your data," Heren said. "The fauna on this planet aren't very large, but they're tough and very fast. Their biome's got plenty of power, after all. They avoid anything our size, but they could destroy that little thing without even trying. Then there's the fungi. Spores grow on *everything*."

"Fortunately, I've plenty of bots. We'll drop this many at every tree we visit," Errant told her.

Some of the bots went up the trunk, where their surfaces glittered against the abyssal black, and some began burrowing into the bare ground. Besides the dark trees, Midnight was shockingly short on anything that looked like plant life: no dark shrubs or grasses, no competing species that used the same light-absorbing technique to feed itself. The terrain's varied color came instead from the fungi. The report from the planet's initial survey team, before PD had staked a claim on Midnight, suggested that not just the giant webs, but an uncounted array of other spores infested the planet's soil.

Errant looked across the landscape, from one distant trunk to another. PD's pipe map showed even spokes stretched across half the small planet's surface, meeting in a point at the heartwood reservoir. He'd assumed that they'd chosen to tap only those trees that happened to stand isolated—but it looked as if the pipes' spacing followed the trees'. It was like they'd been laid out by some vanished park architect or farmer.

He was about to turn away, when sudden movement caught his eye. "What was that?"

"Elda?" Heren was staring at the point where the horizon had *shifted*, where the curve of a hillock humped up instead of sloping down. "Query Second Station. David's monitoring the pipeline grid right now. Anything go out of alignment?"

Fear rinsed through Errant's gut as he trailed Heren's hurried steps back to the shuttle, listened to Elda relaying the question.

Then there was quiet as they climbed back through the airlock—as Elda presumably listened to the response from the power station. Errant tried to lengthen his breaths and not think about the footage he'd seen in his research, images of the first station's wreckage, of the scorched remains of its inhabitants. *It just went*, Heren had said in her debrief. He wondered what Stephen would do if he died here, at the foot of an exploding tree on planet Midnight. *Probably cry into the shoulder of the next sucker.*

Elda said, "Right." She looked up as they reemerged into the shuttle's cockpit, nodded at Heren, who already had her faceplate open. Errant hurried to do the same and caught the tail end of a report.

"—a few centimeters' shift on Foxtrot 7 line, but it doesn't look like anything the struts can't adjust to." Errant recognized the voice of Heren's second-in-command David, tinny over the ship's cheap speakers. "We can move that line up in the check rotation, but I don't think it'll be a problem. Looks like that hill migration mostly missed the grid."

Heren sighed. "Copy. We'll move to the next tree." She had lost the urgency that propelled her towards the ship, and Elda looked as phlegmatic as ever. Errant imagined they could hear his heart trying to pound its way out through his breastbone. He tried his question again.

"What was that?" He hoped it wasn't something he'd read about and forgotten.

Heren gave him a look he couldn't read, all tight eyebrows and narrow eyes. Then she said, "The ground shifts here. Maybe better to say it swells and sinks. We have to keep a tight inspection and maintenance schedule all along the pipelines, to make sure there aren't interruptions to the flow."

That definitely hadn't been in the reports. Errant tried to fit this new and disturbing piece of information into what he knew. "It's not the tapping activity that causes the groundswells?"

Heren shrugged. "It happens near tapped trees, and near untapped ones. It's like everything else. There's no clear correlation. That's why..." She shrugged her next words away. "That's everything PD's tame scientists bothered to figure out."

Errant couldn't tell if she was challenging him to do better, or finding another way to tell him his efforts were useless. He looked away and out the window as the planet's surface fell away again. "This is a strange place."

"I'm not used to it," Heren said, "and I've been here longer than anyone still alive."

It took hours to drop the rest of the bots. At least there were no more sudden groundswells, although Errant turned a new, sharper eye to the folds and humps of earth around the trees they visited. Night had overtaken them and masked the trees' impenetrable shadows by the time they got back to the station, a warren of prefabbed bubbles half dug into the planet's surface. It was farther than the ruins of the first station from the reservoir full of molten heartwood. Whether that was a safe distance or not—well, he was supposed to find out, wasn't he? Errant shivered as he crowded into the airlock-shower with Heren and Elda.

The rinse in the airlock, Heren had told him when he first arrived, was because of the fungi. Even with it, interior walls and air filters clogged with wayward spores and required regular scrub-downs, no matter how tight they kept the seals. "It's a whole pain to delegate half my on-duty people to housework each shift," she'd said with a shrug. Errant had noticed the yeasty-metallic tang in the air when he'd first landed, but that same early survey had established with certainty that the biome's fungal inhabitants were nontoxic. Cygni would never have designated the planet open for companies to claim, if they hadn't.

Inside, Heren went to confer with her on-duty crew and Elda turned her back on him. Errant retreated to the bunk-sized closet that counted as visitor's quarters.

He tried not to take it personally. He was an outsider, a tenderfoot who couldn't really understand tapper life, even if he hadn't been from Cygni. Still, it was lonely.

It was too early to check the data streams from the bots. Without fully meaning to, he opened his terminal and pulled up Stephen's most recent message one more time. Familiarity, guilt, his better judgement, none of it stopped the toxic mixture of warmth and dread, longing and resentment, that flooded him at the sight of Stephen's hollow-cheeked, handsome face. He listened again to the latest earnest, full-hearted, meaningless apology.

I know I keep doing this. I know you have no reason to forgive me or want to see me again. I'm broken. I know it. The times when I'm with you are the only—

The door alert pinged. Errant snapped the file closed, feeling like he'd been caught indecent. He scrubbed at his cheeks, as if he could smooth some of their heat away, and then released the hatch. It was Heren.

She hesitated, as guilty-looking as he felt. It took a moment to unsnarl himself from his irrelevant emotions, to remind himself about exploding trees, and hazardous work conditions, and Heren's ambiguous responses. "Hello, Supervisor. Can I help you with anything?"

"Can I come in?" She actually glanced over her shoulder. Errant wondered if this was a proposition, thought about trying to head her off... *I'm sorry, ma'am, I'm currently in a decaying orbit around a relationship black hole named Stephen...* Then she looked back at him and killed that notion with her next words. "I'd like to make sure of your report."

She wasn't a big woman, out of her environment suit, but her intensity took up its own space between them. He hadn't pegged Heren for a company stooge, but she was in charge here, on an empty planet...

"Of course," he said slowly, and let her inside.

Heren didn't make him feel any better once the door was closed. She kept standing, arms stiff and fists clenched at her sides, the way they'd been out by the tree. There wasn't enough room to back away from her.

Finally, she said, "I sent the message to Cygni."

"Wha—" The implications of her razor-wire tension and furtive aspect grew evolved into new patterns. "Oh—that's—okay." Errant took a deep breath, bottled up the urge to begin bombarding her with questions. "Is there—is there anything you'd like to add to that initial report?"

The anonymous alert had been a simple text file, without much more than the bare outlines of PD's Midnight operation: The company had to build a second power station because the first had been destroyed in an accident; the operation had a shocking mortality rate, even for a frontier project.

Heren closed her eyes, then opened them. He *saw* her walls buckle, her expression melt into grief and pain. "You have to make them pay. Your report, whatever those little bots dig up from the fungi-soil and the trees, that work needs to damn Positive Delta. Burn them to ashes."

Errant swallowed against the urge to make some promise, to make her feel better. Meaningless words wouldn't wipe away her suffering. "If you believe the company is at fault, why did you send your tip anonymously? Testimony from an employee, especially one who," he hesitated, "who has direct experience of the dangers, would be the strongest voice in an argument for reckless endangerment."

"And give them an easy target?" Heren demanded. "They could have sent me on my way before you even got here. And how could I know they wouldn't buy whoever Cygni sent out? I had to see that you actually wanted to know what happened— and I'm still taking a risk. It's always easier to fault the workers. We must have made mistakes. We can't have followed all their oh-so-carefully-researched guidelines." She took a breath, settling herself. "PD could use whatever you write to axe me *and* my people. Then they'll say they've fixed the problem on the ground, and carry on making money with a new crop of desperate hires. There are *always* more desperate hires."

She wasn't wrong. Even Cygni's reach was limited. The report would need a convincing argument about the causes of the explosions here on Midnight, to have a hope of making the Positive Delta admit wrongdoing or change their policies.

"Alright," Errant said. "Let's start by going back over what happened before.

I'm sorry; I know this will be painful, remembering—"

"Oh, don't worry." Heren's lips stretched in a not-smile. "I'm always remembering. You don't forget coming back from patrol to find a crater where your people should be."

At least Heren's testimony drove Stephen and his messages out of Errant's head. Over the next few days, as he watched the data streams from his bots and began playing with different analysis programs, he kept hearing her words again.

The explosion traveled down the line from the reservoir... They made me sift my people's bones from the 'valuable' wreckage so that they could start over.... Some of them we never found. The ground shifted and they were gone.

It wasn't just the horror of it though, the way her face went from pain to rage to uncanny stiffness and back again as she talked. He also kept thinking about the groundswells and earth movements. It was weird. The planetary survey hadn't found tectonic activity, and this movement was smaller-scale anyway—

more like something caused by burrowing animals or the shifts of defrosting soil.

His feelings about the strangeness of the data set grew, the more bots he placed in the field, and the longer he looked at what they gathered. There was *a lot* of information: vast and complex chemical mixtures, spikes of electrical activity. He sat for hours in Second Station's mess, out of the way of most of the tappers, trying and failing to make sense of it.

He had closed his eyes in the face of the ever-growing bulk of information, and was rubbing the heels of his hands against his forehead, when his terminal bleated: the alert for an incoming message, coded personal. Errant swore.

"That bad?" Elda stood in the doorway. He blinked at her. He'd gotten so used to the tappers' stonewalling that he barely noticed when they skirted him. But it seemed silent Elda, of all people, softened at the sight of his self-pity.

"Not how I treat mail from home," she said with a shrug.

"Oh—no." He shook his head, reminded again how isolated they were here. "It's just—I can guess who it's from." No one else would ignore his out-of-system auto-response, would pretend he wasn't busy and working and just completely fed up....

Elda raised an eyebrow. His own words slipped over each other into her silence. "I don't—I don't know what to do. He's toxic, but he needs me, or he needs *somebody*, and every time I see him, it's like the reasonable part of my brain just fades away..." He forced himself to stop, mortified. "Sorry."

She just nodded. "Pheromones, probably."

"Huh?"

"There's no logic to it, but there's a feeling. Something you get from him. Or something he gets from you." She served herself a bowl of vat-protein and rehydrated starches, dug a spoon in, licked it. "I've been there. Sorry to hear it." She sat down with her back to him; conversation concluded.

Elda's presence gave him the discipline not to immediately open Stephen's message. Instead, he went back to staring at the data. Something she'd said niggled. *Pheromones....*

He added another factor to the program he'd been running, watched the patterns of analysis reshape themselves.

The idea was far-fetched, improbable. If he'd been working with a team, he would have been embarrassed to even suggest it —but once it had occurred to him, he couldn't let it go. Instead, the notion gained weight and substance as the bots' output kept accumulating.

He was almost ready to risk his theory to a recording when another tree blew up.

The shockwave ripped through the earth and shook the station habitat. Errant scrambled to his feet as people who'd been off-shift flooded into the common area, wide-eyed and still in pajamas. The four tappers monitoring the grid were still cupped within their screens, hands flying as they tried to assess the damage.

Heren pushed herself through the press of people and turned to the nearest monitor. "Which one?"

Her eyes didn't leave her screen. "Zed 12."

Everyone started speaking at once. "What—" "No—" "That can't be possi—"

"Alright, then!" Heren shouted them all down. "Cyn, are you sure?"

The monitor nodded. Errant's gut clenched. He didn't remember all the designations, but Zed was the spoke of the pipeline starburst that ran closest to the station.

Someone else was asking questions now. "Any fluctuations beforehand? No warnings?"

He needed to see what his own data showed. He pulled out his handheld, skimmed the feeds. Most bots were still transmitting. The feed from Zed 12 was gone, of course, but what the history of the last few minutes showed—it made his breath go tight. "Wait, Heren!"

Heren glared at him. "What is it? What's causing this?"

"I don't want to jump...." His voice faltered.

"You don't want to jump to conclusions, and what, maybe prevent anyone else from dying?" Heren scoffed. "I don't know why I tried so hard to get you here, if you are going to sit back and take *notes* while trees go up around us—"

"Wait." That was Heren's second, David, bristling and stepping into her space. "Heren, *you* called in Cygni? You risked all our jobs for some data-jockey's writeup?"

"I'd rather that than keep risking your lives!" Emotion broke in Heren's voice, and everyone started talking again.

She was right. He had to choose the clearest path towards safety, too, whatever everyone else thought. "Supervisor?"

Somehow, she heard him amid the hubbub. "Quiet, everyone! I said, quiet!"

Errant spoke into the grudging silence. "I'm not certain, but If I'm right—we should evacuate now."

"You can't wait until you file your report to get us fired—" someone began.

"No." He took a deep breath. "The reports PD sent me. They mentioned the way, when the first power station went up, that there was a series of earlier explosions."

Heren nodded, but David waved that point away, "Yes, but it wasn't like they triggered each other. We don't know why that is. The tap lines between the trees run in parallel. The blasts were isolated by both time and space.

"Yes, but the connection isn't about what happened; it's about what *didn't* happen." Errant looked around at the confused faces, and forged ahead. "All my monitoring points to a lot of activity throughout planet's soil, and I mean *a lot* —electrical and chemical movement in patterns I can barely see the edges of. It's at a level of complexity that suggests advanced processes, things like awareness, communicative movement.

"One thing I did see is that all that faded away from Zed 12, starting a few hours ago, and then dropped down to nothing just before it went up. There are a lot more fading spots right now, around a lot more trees."

A hailstorm of sharp-edged words. "Communications? How could you possibly—"

"—So your little bug bots just set it off —"

"Things were fine until—"

Errant held up his hands. "Please! Cygni sent me because of the explosions, but the problem is really something bigger: *They don't understand how this biome works.* Neither do I, fully, but it looks like there's something here, and it has decided that it's tired of firing warning shots."

There was silence as they all tried to make sense of that.

"You think," Heren said at last. "The trees are *sentient*?"

He knew how it sounded. "It's one possible explanation. There has to be some calculus at work, something driving that level of complex interaction."

"Why would they blow themselves up, then?"

"I don't *know!*" He hefted his handheld, trying to suggest the scope of what it held. "I could walk you through the pointers in my data, explain my bots' readings, but the patterns I'm seeing tell me we don't have time. We need to get out of here. It's not safe."

The pause after his words was full of shifting glances, until Heren asked another question.

"Can you prove it? I mean, really prove it, with hard evidence besides your voice and maybe ours—"

"If we believe you," David muttered.

"—And maybe ours?" she repeated. "Positive Delta's not going to let go of this place, this much energy, if they get any choice in the matter. Say we evacuate now; if PD doesn't accept your report, they'll be back with a new crew soon enough."

She was right. He didn't want her to be; he wanted her to get them all offworld right now. He admitted, "The strongest evidence would be to have some of my mobile collectors with their samples. Physical evidence is much harder to deny —but it's all out in the field. It's too much of a risk to re-collect all the bots."

Heren gave him that same folded-brow look, long and piercing.

Then she lifted her chin, turned to Elda, "You're going to pilot the big shuttle." To her second: "David, you're in charge on the flight out." Other questions started to fill the air, but she kept talking. "Inspector Errant. I'll ride with you, and before we leave, we're going to retrieve at least some of your little bots."

The flurry of evacuation passed Errant by. He didn't want to think about what was coming next, so he stared at the data feeds. Energy signatures kept fluctuating and spiking among the roots of every tree he had monitored. It could well be the cadence of a language he had no tools to translate—but even if that was true, there was much he still didn't understand, much that still didn't make sense.

He and Heren sat in the shuttle as the station's emergency evacuation craft lifted off. Heren spoke up on the common channel. "Good speed, people."

There was no response from the bigger ship. It rose and dwindled in the purple-grey sky, and Heren woke the shuttle's engines.

"Where to?"

He checked his handheld one more time. "Go west-southwest, along pipeline Bravo. It looks the most stable right now."

Even with the shuttle at its maximum velocity, the nearest tree was long minutes away. Heren, bent over the controls, spoke without looking at him. "So, will Positive Delta face sanctions for reckless endangerment after all this?"

Errant tried to visualize the shape of his completed report. "Probably not. If it's a new sentient species, Cygni will start assessing Midnight's planetary sovereignty before they rule on how PD was running this harvesting operation. Findings about worker treatment may get lost in the shuffle."

"The fuck you say." The yoke twitched under Heren's hands, and the entire shuttle shuddered. "PD kept us here when the trees started *exploding*. An *entire station* was destroyed. They don't get to treat that like nothing."

Errant cringed at the swooping flight, at his own helplessness. Memories of Stephen intruded suddenly—this trapped feeling was the same as the worst of their fights. He tried, as he had then, to find the words that would move the other person. "I know it's not what you want, but it does stymie them. What's at stake here, now, what we could prove, is bigger than showing what went wrong before. An intelligent species—that's a discovery that changes things. There'll be more research, different regulations on the planet, xenolinguists and biologists coming in to try to understand them—if we ever figure out how to approach them without triggering more tree explosions. Positive Delta certainly won't be able to harvest energy here any time soon; maybe not ever again."

Heren's hands steadied on the controls, but her voice didn't. "You know my crew all hate me now? I just put them out of a job. You've got to be desperate to take one like this, and they were good at it. They're just as good as Soren and Ida and the rest of my first crew. Just as disposable."

She paused, and Errant saw her throat work. "I could have taken the company's hush money. They offered a ride out of

here, early retirement after the accident—
but they shouldn't get to just keep going."

"They won't—" Errant tried to say, but
his terminal interrupted him with a
shrilled warning and, while the tone still
jangled the air of the cockpit, an explosion
bloomed, blue-white and closer than the
horizon's line.

Errant clung to his seat. "Do you think
we should—"

Heren angled the skimmer's nose
down. "We're coming up on Bravo 1. Do
your readings say we can land?"

They bounced down by a tree that looked
just like the first he'd visited. Errant
forced muscles knotted in anticipation of
another eruption to unclench. Out of the
shuttle, across the meaningless line, he
dropped down at the foot of the tree. His
fingers were clumsy in their gloves, but
they managed to scoop up three of the
bots, which had responded to his recall
command and swum up out of the earth.

He hesitated, scanning the data feeds.
There were a handful more bots
converging on this point. He looked out
across Midnight's lonely terrain. It looked

like there were more of the pale fungal webs now, more uneven swells across the landscape. The sight shifted something in his mind, in the way his thoughts worried over the data.

Something you need, Elda had said. What did the trees need? What did they have? What—or who—had the agency here?

"Errant." Heren hadn't left the shuttle. "Can this tree *see* or feel us here?"

"It's not the trees," Errant said. The nearest bot was seconds away. "It's the mycelial network."

"What?"

"The mycelial network," he repeated, "the fungus system that connects the trees underground. It must somehow draw off the excess energy the trees absorb—that's how they don't overheat—and it diverts minerals from the soil to them. How else could those trees get enough nutrition, without other plant-equivalent growth around?" He shivered, thinking of the network beneath them, a mass of impulses, awareness, and intentions woven into the earth and through the roots of the dark tree, wicking away its overburden of energy and subtly directing its growth.

"How does that even—" Heren began.

Then the data feed from the incoming bot—from all his bots—disappeared. The earth beneath his feet shivered, even as he pushed himself up and into motion.

"Come on!" Heren shouted as he stumbled forward. The ground bucked and white filaments spread around him like starbursts.

He threw himself into the shuttle's airlock. The engine raced, but he felt no lift.

Heren swore. "Something's caught—"

Errant made it to his seat in the cockpit as she fought with the controls, finally rotating the thrusters and gunning them to rip free of the filaments that had seized the landing feet. The shuttle leapt from the ground.

The air around the ship turned to fire as the tree went up beneath them and the shockwave threatened to knock them out of the sky. Heren stayed glued to the controls, leaning forward as if she could will the ship faster. Gravity dug its claws into Errant's bones and flesh as the shuttle shot upwards on a steep trajectory.

"The whole grid is going," Errant didn't have the bot data anymore, but he could watch the feeds from Midnight's human-made structures disappear one by one. "That's the reservoir. That's the station." He imagined the web of explosions spreading across the planet's surface beneath, all that pent-up energy released in a great, cleansing rush.

The shuttle's engine strained, and then the cockpit's viewscreen turned black and bloomed with stars. Another few moments of pressure, and the gee forces of acceleration fell away, leaving them in the calm of freefall.

Errant had a new, uncomfortable thought.

"Can this ship do interplanetary distances?" His Cygni transport wouldn't be back in system for another five standard days.

Heren made a noncommittal noise. "Not officially. We'll make it to the relay station, though. That's where the escape craft was headed."

"Oh. Will you meet your crew there?" He saw her expression change, and regretted the words.

"Former crew." The bitterness was back in her tone. "They won't want to see me. Besides, I think I should stick with you for now. Go on record about everything I saw and did at Midnight's stations, the first one and the second." She gave him a smile that was almost convincing. "That has to count for something, right?"

"We'll make PD feel it," Errant promised her. "And your people will come around."

Heren shrugged. "Maybe. I did betray them."

"I'd hope they see that losing a job is the smaller evil in all this. Hell, if an alien fungus can blow up half its own planet to get rid of its human parasites—" He stopped, afraid that he might have been too flippant in the face of everything she'd been through, but she nodded.

"You have to excise the rotten bits, so they don't kill you."

"Huh." Errant let that idea settle into him for a long moment as they pushed farther into space. "Yes, you really do." Then, because they had some time before they reached the relay station, he pulled up his personal correspondence files on his handheld and deleted some messages that he didn't need respond to.

*See Chloe Smith's story "Midnight's Second
Station" online at Metaphorosis.
If you liked it, leave a comment. Authors love
that!
Remember to subscribe to our e-mail updates so
you'll know when new stories are posted.*

About the story

This story owes its existence to *Entangled Life* by
Merlin Sheldrake, the nonfiction book that launched a
thousand spec fic stories—or at least one by every
genre writer I know who's read it. Seriously, though,
it's a mind-opening book, which is completely
appropriate, given that it's all about fungi. I knew I
wanted to write a "mushroom story", but I wasn't
exactly sure what direction to take it, until I read
another nonfiction piece, this one about trees. My
mind caught on a phrase about how chlorophyll
absorbs a limited spectrum of visible light, which is
why it's green. I started thinking about heat and light
absorption, and the blackest-black pigments that
researchers have created, and somehow the dark
trees evolved out of that idea mixture. The human
story of Heren and Errant and corporate malfeasance
only came after I built the setting for them, although I
was able to add Midnight to a wider universe I've used
before. (Readers may remember the Cygni Authority
from my earlier story "Rock-Adda's World", which ran
in *Metaphorosis* in 2021.)

A question for the author

Q: Are you a Luddite? Or do you have the latest and greatest technology?

A: I'm a member of the Oregon Trail generation—the people who got the internet at home when they were children or teens, who know the sound of dial-up, might have gotten their first cell phone when they went off to college, and definitely had social media accounts by the time they graduated. As a result, although I remember life before everything was digitally connected, I've always had to adapt to evolving technology. I try to be comfortable with new platforms, media, and devices, but I also don't value any of it for its own sake. Technology is really just a big umbrella term for an expanding set of tools. Like storytelling, the value is in how it's used.

About the author

Chloe Smith teaches middle-school English and history, which means she had to completely reinvent her job in 2020. She's very glad to be back in the classroom now, and spending much less time on Zoom. Besides teaching, she works as a proofreader for *Locus* and *Fantasy* magazines, and writes science fiction and fantasy stories whenever she can make the time. She was born and raised in the San Francisco Bay Area, and she lived in Texas and Washington states, New York City, and rural France before coming back to California. Her short fiction has appeared in *Metaphorosis, Three-Lobed Burning Eye*, and *Daily Science Fiction*, among other places.

@chloehsmith

Copyright

Title information

Metaphorosis May 2022

ISSN: 2573-136X (online)
ISBN: 978-1-64076-228-2 (e-book)
ISBN: 978-1-64076-229-9 (paperback)

Copyright

Publisher

Metaphorosis
a magazine of speculative fiction

Metaphorosis Magazine is an imprint of
Metaphorosis Publishing
Neskowin, OR, USA

Discounts available

Substantial discounts are available for educational institutions, including writing workshops. Discounts are also available for quantity purchases. For details, contact Metaphorosis at metaphorosis.com/about

Metaphorosis Publishing

Metaphorosis offers beautifully written science fiction and fantasy. Our imprints include:

Metaphorosis Magazine
Plant Based Press
Verdage
Vestige

You can also find us:
@MetaphorosisMag, @MetaphorosisRev, @Metaphorosis
www.facebook.com/metaphorosis

Help keep Metaphorosis running by supporting us at
Patreon.com/metaphorosis

See more about some of our books on the following pages.

Metaphorosis

a magazine of speculative fiction

Metaphorosis is an online speculative fiction magazine dedicated to quality writing. We publish an original story every week, along with author bios, interviews, and notes on story origins.

We also publish monthly print and e-book issues, as well as yearly Best of and Complete anthologies.

Come and see us online at magazine.Metaphorosis.com.

Plant Based Press

plant
based
press

Vegan-friendly science fiction and fantasy, including anthologies of the year's best SFF stories, from 2016-2020.

Chambers of the Heart
speculative stories
by
B. Morris Allen

A heart that's a building, a dog that's a program, a woman sinking irretrievably — stories about love, loss, and movement.

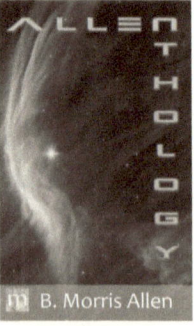

Susurrus

A darkly romantic story of magic, love, and suffering.

Allenthology: Volume I

Including three full collections of SFF stories.

Verdage

Science fiction and fantasy books for writers – full of great stories, often with an additional focus on the craft of speculative fiction writing.

Reading 5X5 x2

Duets

How do authors' voices change when they collaborate?

A round-robin of five talented science fiction and fantasy authors collaborating with each other and writing solo.

Including stories by Evan Marcroft, David Gallay, J. Tynan Burke, L'Erin Ogle, and Douglas Anstruther.

Score

an SFF symphony

An anthology with an emotional score from the heights of joy to the depths of despair – but always with a little hope shining through.

Reading 5X5

Five stories, five times

See how different writers take on the same material.

Reading 5X5

Writers' Edition

Two extra stories, the story seed, and authors' notes on writing.

Vestige

Novelettes, novellas, and novels by Metaphorosis authors.

The Nocturnals
Mariah Montoya

Night is Dangerous.
Day is deadly.

Where day and night last thirty years, humans move constantly stay ahead of the night and cruel Nocturnals that call it home. But a boy is lost out there.

www.ingramcontent.com/pod-product-compliance
Lightning Source LLC
Chambersburg PA
CBHW050449110726
47899CB00003B/864